MW01156835

The
PIANIST IN
THE DARK

MICHÈLE HALBERSTADT

PEGASUS BOOKS

NEW YORK

To Laurent Bonelli
my little prince

THE PIANIST IN THE DARK

Pegasus Books LLC
80 Broad St., 5th Floor
New York, NY 10004

Copyright © Michèle Halberstadt, Éditions Albin Michel, 2008

First Pegasus Books edition 2011

Interior design by Maria Fernandez

Library of Congress Cataloging-in-Publication Data is available.

ISBN: 978-1-60598-118-5

10 9 8 7 6 5 4 3 2 1

Printed in the United States of America
Distributed by W. W. Norton & Company, Inc.
www.pegasusbooks.us

But the fool on the hill
Feels the sun coming down
And the eyes in his head
See the world spinning round

—The Beatles

Chapter 1

SHE DOESN'T KNOW THE COLOR OF THE SKY OR THE shape of the clouds, doesn't know the meaning of blue or red, of dark or pale. She lives in blackness. This is the word they have given to what she describes. She can make out light by its heat, its smell, sometimes even its sound: the flickering of a candle, the crackling of fire. She knows that daytime throbs with agitation and that silence awaits nightfall to be heard. Luckily for her, listening is what she does best.

She discerns sounds to which no one lends an ear: the greenhouse pane shuddering in its frame when the west wind blows;

the cat's tongue scraping its coat as it licks itself clean. She has never mistaken a sharp for a flat, a wood pigeon for a turtledove. What stirs her blood are the nuances—the spectrum of sounds, the scale of emotions. She can differentiate between alarm and fear, between a gust and a breeze, between courtesy and sincerity, between allegro and allegretto. She feels, she quivers. She vibrates, trembles, shivers.

She blushes as well.

She hopes she is pretty but is not reassured by the sympathies she elicits from her visitors. How can they be trusted? They are blinded by the pity she inspires. A young woman sitting before her musical instrument makes for a fetching image. She imagines it, composes it behind her eyelids. It could be the name of a painting. "Young Woman at the Piano." But for the painting to work, the woman in question must be attractive.

She remembers when her father overheard her timidly asking Nina, the chambermaid, "Would you say I'm pretty?"—how he rushed out from the drawing room, placed his daughter's hands around Nina's ample hips, then around her own, and murmured: "You're so delicate, your hands almost fit around your waist." The pride she felt just then rippled through her body like a wave of heat.

So, she is delicate. With a pleasant figure. She has long, thick hair that Nina confines in a silk net to keep it out of her face. It stays hidden behind her neck, the low bun growing heavier as the day wears on. Her cheeks seem soft to the touch, her straight nose a bit long, her mouth full, lips chapped because she nibbles at them then tries in vain to relieve the burning with a flick of the tongue.

She is proud of her slender fingers, the nails, cut short, which she polishes every day before feeling for the flowers engraved around the lock on the piano lid, the key to which never leaves her pocket.

It is her piano, hers and hers alone.

She has locked her world inside it. Seven notes that can segue into infinity for those who take the pains to master them. For her it was not about pain, but suffering. She should hate that instrument, symbol of a world that abruptly turned its back on her. Still, she plays tirelessly, her eyes open like two crystals that no longer reflect a thing, neither curves nor colors. Her gaze has been blank, like a window with its shutters closed, since that wooly morning she woke up blind.

Can anyone remember anything from the age of three? Her first memory is of loss, fear.

She wakes up and does not recognize anything. The world around her is a dark blur. When she reaches out her hand, the candle flame burns it. She lets out a piercing scream, but not of pain. Her terror is absolute. She senses the candle but cannot see it. She knows she should be able to discern its flickering glow, yet nothing emerges from the obscurity that has engulfed her. She turns around, gropes in her bed, finds the piece of bluish satin that she rolls around her thumb to fall asleep. The cloth has lost its shimmer. It is just another ominous element in the blackness that has erased everything from her room. She screams.

People come rushing in. She recognizes them only by their voices, their scents. Her father's hoarse, quivering pitch; the starch that perfumes Nina's apron and the freshness of her soothing hands; her mother's hysterical wails and warm tears that dampen the piece of satin she sucks on as she rocks to a nursery rhyme only she can hear. Trying to soothe the fear, to tame the darkness that has swallowed her since she woke.

Topsy-turvy. Everyone around her is thrust into an emotional vortex. They try to escape, they flail about, they run in circles. Frenzied footsteps, doors slamming shut, servants scurrying about, windows bursting open, shouts to have the carriage prepared; then hoofs banging on the cobblestone, whips snapping at manes, horses galloping a few streets away to fetch Herr Stolz, the family doctor—his heavy, muffled footsteps in her bedroom, the clanking of cold instruments he removes from his bag, the warm compresses he instructs Nina to hold against her eyelids till they burn, the steam baths, the salves, the ointments. Nothing works. Neither silence nor noise. Neither cold nor heat. Nor prayers, nor tears, nor science, nor medicine. Neither her mother's pleading nor Nina's hands.

Eight days later, the news had made its way around Vienna. Maria Theresia von Paradis, the only child of the Imperial Secretary to the Empress, has lost her sight.

Chapter 2

SHE PLAYED THE PIANO BEFORE. OR RATHER, SHE loved to put her fingers on the keys that seemed disproportionately large beneath her tiny hands. Especially the long black ones, higher than the white ones, slimmer, more mysterious as well. Though a black key alone is of little interest, it can transform the sonority of a white one: accentuate its lightness, underscore its melancholy.

The wooden piano in the parlor had always been her refuge, her favorite toy. She considers that she had mastered music before language. As a matter of fact, she sang her first word. She hated it when the cat would sit on the edge of the piano lid. She would tell him to "Get down!" "*Runter!*" she would say. But he scared her a bit, so she softened the imperative, finessing it into two notes— D, E. "Runter" became the nickname of poor Hanz, who at the age of twelve had to get used to this new appellation.

Her days are now invariably spent behind a piano. When she practices or gives a concert, it is on the stately grand piano that proudly dominates the large drawing room. But when she can get away and play for herself, when she wants to improvise, compose, rant and rave, confide in herself, assuage the vehemence she keeps bottled up, it is on the piano that Runter no longer dares approach. She has the only key that opens it, but she knows that it is in fact the piano which holds the key to her dreams, her turmoil. It is a diary full of feelings she refuses to share with anyone, feelings she smothers by keeping them to herself. Only the piano of her childhood knows her secrets.

The yellow of the candle, the blue of the satin, the off-white of the milk that left the yummy mustache on her upper lip—these are the only colors etched in her memory. She knows that the sun looks like the candle, the sky like the cloth, the piano keys like the color of milk. She has forgotten all the others. Red, green, orange, purple—they mean nothing to her. They are words devoid of meaning. So she has turned them into notes. Red is vivid, thus G-sharp. Green is a soft shade: F. Orange is conspicuous: E. Purple is more discreet: C-flat. And to the color of the wood framing her piano she has given her favorite note: C.

She is no longer frustrated to have lost a sense the appeal of which she has forgotten. What is sight, exactly? To know what everyday objects look like? A table, a chair, a mirror? But she knows better than anyone, in her own way, and this way suits her. Her father, who puts her piano stool in its place every morning, for example, has no idea that the front left leg squeaks each time she leans forward to hit one of the pedals. Has Nina, who cleans the large chest of drawers in her room every day, ever noticed that the paint is flaking from under the ledge and that the unvarnished wood is visible? No one really knows at what they look. Yet she, with her ear that attends the slightest quivering of the air, her fingers that question every object they touch, her sense of smell that is so keenly developed she can predict what the weather will be in three days—she knows she is nobody's fool.

With time, she has persuaded herself that sight is an illusion that leads the other senses astray, renders them ineffective. Whereas hers are always alert. Blind? What's the fuss? She lives in another world and she likes it there.

Alas, this is something her father cannot accept.

Joseph Anton, secretary to Their Majesties, expressed his gratitude to the Empress by naming his daughter after her, and the excessive love he bore his child would make his wife jealous her whole life long. He who exclaimed upon discovering his new-born: "The fairies of beauty and talent have blessed this child!", he, the influential diplomat whose advice is sought by the members of the Court, who is privileged to see Their Majesties every day, for whom nothing is more important than social status, whose comely wife gave him a daughter of unmistakable beauty—he who has been refused nothing cannot admit that fate has played such a nasty trick on him.

His daughter must be cured. It is his wish.

So while music teachers instructed Maria Theresia in song and harmony, men of science turned her into their guinea pig, alternating bloodletting with purges and cauteries, putting leeches on her eyelids, confining her head to cataplasms for days on end, and even trying a new discovery: electrical seizure induction. So painful were the treatments that new symptoms soon appeared: nervous trembling, attacks of panic, uncontrollable sobbing at dusk—and the blindness never diminished. By the time Joseph Anton admitted that the various procedures to which his daughter was submitted only made her worse, he had succeeded in weakening both her health and her nerves.

At seventeen, Mademoiselle Paradis, born a child prodigy and blind soon after, passionate and docile, had grown into a graceful young adult with sophisticated manners—a reputed virtuoso pianist who, behind her beautiful and smooth face, hides the violent torments of a troubled, melancholic temperament. She knows she is misunderstood, feels unloved, and trusts no one.

The Empress made Maria Theresia her protégée because she appreciated her father and sympathized with his misfortune. And even if she was not her godmother, she felt responsible for this child who bore her name—all the more because of her remarkable musical talent. To confirm her own persuasion in that regard, the Empress entrusted the child at age five to Georg Christoph Wagenseil, her personal musical counselor and the official composer to the Court. This famous pianist taught harpsichord to a handful of pupils from Viennese high society. Struck by her talent, he recommended her to Herr Kotzeluck to work on piano and to Abbot Vogler, an expert in composition, so she might write her own music. Proud not to have been mistaken about the girl's potential, the Empress decided to bequeath her an annuity of 200 gold ducats. A small fortune managed by Joseph Anton, whose lifestyle flourished proportionately.

The Empress also asked for medical opinions from doctors she respected: the Baron Anton von Stoerck, her private physician; Professor Gustav Barth, a cataract specialist; and even the Baron de Wenzel, a famed Parisian optometrist then living in Vienna. At her request they all examined the child in full and they all concluded that Mademoiselle von Paradis was incurably blind.

They all also agreed on another point, one that categorically contradicted their earlier diagnoses: The child suffered from amaurosis, a form of blindness that appears suddenly without any malfunctioning of the optical system. Its onset is either toxic, congenital, or nervous.

All three physicians were quick to zero in on the third possibility. The search was on, and each of them wanted to find the answer before the others. Thus, what had happened the evening before Maria Theresia woke up blind? What had she seen or heard that affected her so violently as to make her lose her sight?

Having already submitted to barbarous treatments, Maria Theresia was now being harassed by an onslaught of indiscreet questions. Having let them probe her brain and eyes, should she now bare her soul and allow them to rifle through her memories? There was a way out: All she had to do was lie, or at least hide the truth—which is what she did.

Confronted with her silence, doctors and parents gave up questioning her but remained persuaded that something had necessarily occurred—a noise, a murmur, an incident in the doorway—to shock her into lifelong blindness.

Yes, she kept quiet, but what would she have said, had she wished to open up? Nothing had happened. Nothing out of the ordinary. In the middle of the night doors were slammed and voices raised, cries of innocence on the one hand and agonized sobs on the other. At three and a half one doesn't understand the meaning of the words, but one gets the gist of them: Love had disappeared from this house. Over the course of the years, she would learn about her father's anger, his violence as well. As for her mother, she was prone to a rampant hysteria that made her nervous, unpredictable, sometimes scary. Maria Theresia learned not to trust them.

She had the impression that her illness brought everything to the fore. Her blindness was at once the principal cause of their fighting—her parents were far from being of the same mind as to what treatments to try—and the underlying foundation of their union, as if besides her, they had nothing in common. Nothing but the love they bore her—a love that was suffocating, oppressive, even blinding.

She felt that being blind was the only power she had over them. She was the object of their obsession, the subject of their confrontations, but without her, her blindness, they would have nothing to discuss. Her handicap freed her from her parents and at the same time enabled the three of them to remain a family.

Chapter 3

H E DOESN'T KNOW FRUSTRATION OR THE BITTERNESS of failure. His life has always been forged by good fortune. Son of a reputed huntsman, he catches, during an outing, the attention of the Archbishop of Constance, who decides to have him schooled. Ziegler, the Kapellmeister, teaches him recorder, cello, and organ. From the Jesuits of Dillingen he learns mathematics and physics. Raised at one with nature, he shows talent as a water diviner and a healer. He arrives in Vienna at the age of thirty-three already a doctor in theology, philosophy, and law. But he intends to devote himself to medicine, which he studies under the aegis of, among others, Professor Stoerk, the Empress's personal physician.

Taking up an interest in the occult sciences, he writes his doctoral thesis on "The Influence of the Planets on the Human Body" and becomes a Freemason, thus securing himself a network of influential acquaintances.

In 1768, at the age of thirty-four, he holds many diplomas and has proven his musical talent. He has great presence. A full head taller than most of his contemporaries, he possesses a certain elegance, entrancing light blue eyes, and a soft voice. He exudes calm and goodwill. Men seek out his company. He is pleasing to women. Everyone praises his kindliness, his wit—sharp but never biting—and gallantry, his good upbringing. In short, he is a man out of the ordinary, cultivated, and excellent company.

In reality, Franz Anton Mesmer is all of the above, only less appealingly so. He is detached rather than enthusiastic, tenacious rather than enterprising. More ambitious than his careful display of modesty suggests. His low birth branded him for life, and excess of pride has weakened him. He has convictions— passions, even—but he expects them to be both recognized and lucrative. His sincerity is diminished by his unquenchable desire to be recognized and admitted into Viennese high society. For that he will do almost anything. His quest for social status is his Achilles' heel.

Franz Anton Mesmer gave up on love the day he married Maria Anna von Eulenschenk, widow of a former Secretary of

Finance, Baron von Bosch. She is one of the richest women in the capital. She is ten years older than Mesmer and has a teenage son. Sophisticated and still beautiful, she appreciates the arts and music. She admires Mesmer for the breadth of his accomplishments and his numerous talents. He is exhilarated by the interest she shows him, and he truly believes that the pleasure each takes in the other's company will be enough to create a lasting bond. He finds her physically graceful and elegant. He values the image they shape as a couple, his height a perfect match for her daintiness. They make a striking pair. He likes that.

Sex doesn't interest him. Having rebuffed the advances of several priests in his youth, he never felt, with the women enamored of him, enough pleasure to trigger an insatiable desire to repeat the experience again and again. He enjoys the power that he feels during the sexual act more than he does the act itself. In truth, he is indifferent to physical love, and Maria Anna is not herself overly preoccupied with what the Jesuits call the "devils of the flesh." Their alliance is Mesmer's triumph, the finishing touch on an edifice carefully constructed over the years. The poor boy from Germany destined for the priesthood has become a person routinely received in Court, one of the city's most powerful men and envied figures.

Now that he is rich, Mesmer can give free rein to philanthropic pursuits. He expresses his sincere curiosity in regard to the arts and artists with pomp. His address—261 Landstrasse, the imposing home of the late Secretary of Finance—has become a hub of Viennese intellectual and cultural life. A sort of small Versailles on the Danube, the sumptuous property offers two guesthouses overlooking a garden. You can walk down shaded paths lined with antique statues and fountains. On the far side of a grove are a dovecote and an aviary. And if you venture further, you reach a gazebo that overlooks the Prater and affords an unobstructed view of the city. But what delights Mesmer most is an enchanting open-air theater with a bandstand on each side. Actors and musicians, professional and amateur, perform on the outdoor stage. Mesmer himself often plays in the orchestra. His entertaining and eloquent dinner conversation is as popular as the shows and the concerts. He fascinates and intrigues the aristocracy. He has quickly become all the rage.

It was at this small theater on October 1, 1768, that Mozart, who had just been refused a commission on which his father Leopold was counting, first performed *Bastien and Bastienne*, which Mesmer had sponsored.

As the story goes, at the end of the performance, a nine-year-old blind pianist offered the composer a bouquet of flowers. There was only a three-year age difference between them. They would become friends—he would later dedicate a concerto to her. That evening, unbeknownst to both of them, Mesmer and Maria Theresia crossed paths without meeting.

Chapter 4

HER FATHER HAD PROMISED TO PUT AN END TO ALL attempts to cure her. It was on May 15, 1776, the day she turned seventeen. She was fiddling with the gift he had placed on her napkin during lunch: a small sack, silky and rough like her heavy bedroom curtains—a material called velvet. She felt its weight without undoing the drawstring. She guessed what might be inside: a ring, a broach, a pair of earrings, a necklace—one of those gifts she called "selfish presents": finery that is pleasing to the eye, for those who can see. Her father's way of showing his daughter off and compensating for the handicap that so distressed him. She took no pleasure in bedecking herself with these objects designed to make those who wear them sparkle. Why shine a light on a young woman whose eyes are dead to the world? She would have preferred a bouquet of peonies with their intoxicating smell, or a pair of thin gloves for her constantly cold fingertips, or even a fur muff.

She could sense her father's impatience by his breathing, which always grew heavier when he tried to contain himself.

She put down the sack without attempting to open it.

"Thank you for the generous gift. I'll open it when I'm alone. I can best appreciate things in silence and solitude."

She paused to let her mother try, unsuccessfully, to restrain an exasperated sigh. Then turning to her father, she picked up where she had left off.

"The gift I want most won't cost you a thing. On the contrary, it will allow you to cut back on the enormous expenses my health has caused you. What I wish more than anything is to stop having to see all these different specialists. Not one of them has been able to explain what stopped my eyes from seeing. But instead of admitting defeat, they've taken it out on my body. They've assaulted my brain and left me a bundle of nerves. Incessant migraines; burning eyelids, as if salt's been thrown on them; eczema gnawing at my scalp, making me lash out like a pony shaking off flies—the doctors have brought illness upon illness on me but have never treated the one they were originally called in for. So I'll say it once and for all: I am satisfied with my lot. I enjoy flattering you by wearing the jewelry you've chosen for me. But I beg of you: Think of me and not yourself."

A silver platter crashed to the floor, startling them and interrupting a tirade embarrassing for her parents but not for her. The noise brought a smile to Maria Theresia's lips. Dear Nina, trying as always to restore peace and to keep up the appearances of a festive lunch. A quartet of violinists were waiting in the kitchen, preparing to celebrate the birthday joyfully. Maria Theresia heard them tuning their instruments and thought she could make out the overture to *Le donne letterate,* the opera buffa by Salieri, her singing and composition professor. She raised her glass of white wine in their direction as they were walking across the immense living room to the podium set up under the crystal chandelier.

"To the peace of my body and mind!"

She then took her father by his hand when he came to stroke hers. She squeezed it with all her strength until he murmured:

"You have my word."

Chapter 5

A FEW WEEKS LATER THE THREE OF THEM ATTENDED a concert at the house in the Landstrasse. In June Franz Anton Mesmer had acquired a little-known instrument composed of glass bowls that were filled to various levels with water and with which musical tones were created by means of friction. He excelled at playing his glass-harmonica, which was considered one of the most beautiful of its kind. The word spread like wildfire in the capital: One simply had to hear the sound that Mesmer called "the source of harmony among men." The Viennese prided themselves on their ear for music, and Mesmer's solo variations became the must-see show of the summer.

Although perfectly devoid of any artistic curiosity herself, Nina was thrilled that Maria Theresia was going. For the host of the evening inspired in Nina the kind of irrational admiration that a celebrity can in someone pure of heart. Simply because a man is handsome and basks in the flattering glow of his era, people project onto him qualities that he does not necessarily possess but which nonetheless justify the superlatives used to describe him. So Nina saw to it that her mistress's low bun softened the sliver of her profile, that the mauve in her dress enhanced her pearl-white complexion and the bodice accented her slim waist, and that her feet were perfectly arched. It was like playing with dolls, creating a woman able to attract a man of Mesmer's caliber. Nina was not worried about Maria Theresia's blindness. As she explained to her mistress, a woman's vulnerabilities render her all the more attractive. That evening Maria Theresia started to grasp some of the nuances of the word "femininity."

The Paradises were not accustomed to visiting Mesmer's house. Over the years their host had established his reputation as musician/patron of the arts to such an extent that Mozart, before setting off for Paris, had asked him for a letter of introduction to Marie Antoinette, and Mesmer had mentioned this request to Joseph Anton, whose amicable relationship with the Empress Maria Theresia was well-known. The two men thus began to meet. The doctor never missed an opportunity to ask about the Secretary's daughter. At first it was to flatter Paradis by showing interest in the person most dear to him. But by dint of questioning him about the treatments his daughter was receiving and learning of their harmful effects on her physical and mental health, Mesmer ended up offering to treat her himself.

Mesmer had recently succeeded in strengthening his reputation as a visionary in the field of medicine thanks to the care he had administered to a twenty-seven-year-old woman, a friend of his wife's. Franziska von Osterlin suffered from various ills, ranging from violent vomiting to spells of paralysis that variously affected her limbs. She sojourned frequently with the Mesmers. The doctor identified approximately fifteen ills afflicting her and, over the years, managed to cure her of all of them. Gossipmongers claimed that her case interested him only because he hoped to marry her to his wife's son, whom he wanted out of the house. But facts were facts: Fraülein Franziska claimed she was cured, and rumor had it that a happy event would bring her cure to completion.

Since advancing his thesis on celestial bodies, Mesmer had become convinced that a mutual influence existed among the stars, the earth, and human beings. According to him, this influence was transmitted via a fluid that restored the nerves to health.

In 1772, following in the footsteps of Father Hell, a Jesuit astrology professor who prided himself on curing people with magnets, Mesmer adapted his procedure of magnetic healing but soon clashed with the priest. He then pretended to have discovered the method himself and accused Hell of plagiarism.

The following year, when he met a Swiss priest, Father Gassner, who practiced exorcism, Mesmer decided to give up magnets and apply his own hands instead. The former water diviner/healer determined that his body itself was a conduit of the curative fluid, of the energy that relieved the pain engendered by nervous ills.

The case of Maria Theresia arrived at the perfect time. The specialists maintained that her eyes suffered from no scientifically evident disorder. She thus must be unconsciously inflicting the disease on herself. Had the treatments subsequently plunged her further into a melancholia to which she had never before been subject, then? Nervous disorder, no doubt about it.

Mesmer was able to appear persuasive. Such arguments coming from a friend of Mozart's could only be trustworthy. The city was swarming with rumors about him, claiming, for example, that Father Hell's discovery had got stolen—but wasn't this proof of the fascination that Mesmer aroused? Joseph Anton, as a man of influence, was not ignorant of the process that leads from admiration to envy only to materialize in malicious gossip.

Not knowing what to make of this new medicine, Paradis spoke with the Empress's physician, the Baron von Stoerck. Von Stoerck knew Mesmer well. They both came from the same area of Germany and spoke the same dialect. He had had Mesmer as a student and had even agreed to be a witness at his wedding.

The well-meaning advice Paradis received was tinged with the famous Professor's customary irony:

"Mesmer's treatments couldn't harm a fly."

The presence of the Paradis family at Mesmer's concert in his house on Landstrasse owed nothing to chance. But because the young woman's father could not go back on his birthday promise, the offer had to come from Mesmer himself. It was imperative that, upon being introduced to her, he be seized by sudden inspiration.

Chapter 6

MARIA THERESIA WAS UNAWARE OF FRANZ ANTON Mesmer's medical ambitions. All she knew about him was his reputation as a patron of the arts. She had heard him play with orchestras and remembered him as being a mediocre pianist.

But that evening, sitting between her parents on the bandstand near the gazebo at the left side of the garden, she could only admire the quality of his improvisations on the glassharmonica.

Was the instrument responsible for the trembling sonority, or was it his way of playing it? A sense of peace emanated from that assembly of air, glass, and water.

Maria Theresia lifted her head, offering her senses a well-deserved pause. She lost the panicky stiffness she felt when surrounded by strangers whose gazes seemed to pierce through her. She no longer felt weighed down by the baubles that encumbered her neck and earlobes. She felt dizzy, as if a wind had risen and blown right through her. Her hands were quivering as they did sometimes at church when prayers overlapped, as if they were taking a shortcut to heaven.

The concert was over, but she was shaking too much to applaud.

She asked her parents to bring her some cold water.

Her temples were moist. She was shivering.

"I was hoping you might take comfort in the music."

She sensed a figure leaning over. The chairs next to her were empty.

He pulled one toward him and sat facing her.

"Your body's reaction to the sounds of the glass-harmonica is intense. This music affects you because your body torments you. You suffer because you are not in harmony with yourself. The body is an instrument. It needs to be tuned, like piano keys."

His voice was insistent, enveloping. The more he spoke, the more she leaned back, as if he represented a force she couldn't resist.

"Let me take care of you. I'm asking you to allow me this chance. A pianist of your caliber needs peace and quiet. Allow me to offer you a few days' rest from your daily life. You need to breathe without being told how to do so."

She started to shake again, but it was contained within—a muffled vibration that made her heart skip a beat.

"But my parents . . ."

"Your parents want your well-being. I'll be able to persuade them."

She dared lean into the warmth of his breath.

"Are you a magician?"

He let out a hearty laugh.

"No, but I observe you, I see you."

She bit her lips and put her hand on her face so he couldn't read anything into it.

He stood up.

"So it's decided. I'll call on your father tomorrow and ask his permission to have you be my guest for a short time. Mademoiselle . . ."

He disappeared without a sound. She heard only her mother's footsteps as she came to cover her daughter with a shawl.

"Shall we go? This garden is too humid."

"Where is Father?"

"I don't see him. Ah, yes, he's by the fountain speaking with Herr Mesmer."

Maria Theresia stumbled to get up. She felt numb.

Her mother took her by the arm.

"Do you not feel well?"

"I feel . . . lost."

Maria Theresia's lips broke into a slight smile that her mother did not notice.

"But it is not unpleasant."

Chapter 7

WHILE MESMER'S OFFER WAS BEING DISCUSSED—
that is, the time it took for Joseph Anton to convince his wife to listen to reason—and while
Mesmer was preparing the apartments for his future patient,
Maria Theresia had plenty of time to take full measure of what
she was in for.

She had instructed Nina to keep her ears open and now
understood that she had fallen into a trap: Mesmer intended to
cure her. She couldn't bring herself to be angry at him. He had
read her so perspicaciously! She sensed in his interest for her

a truth, an integrity that she never questioned for an instant. She was used to trusting only herself, that is, her own instinct. She had developed an almost nearly perfect ear and a remarkable memory. She could hear in the inflection of a voice whether a person was sincere or affected, and she detected in Mesmer's voice true honesty. Whatever his deeper intentions, she had no reason to doubt the sincerity with which he addressed her.

On the other hand, she didn't trust herself. His rapid insightfulness left her feeling highly emotional. She feared that once she was in his home, the vulnerability to which she had formerly been accustomed would take hold of her again.

Whatever others might think—blinded by a pity that paralyzed them to the point of seeming to be unfeeling—she had managed to transform her handicap into a strength, even a weapon. People became so uncomfortable around the blind that they overdid everything. They spoke too loud, shook hands too forcefully, thrust their faces too close, as if she were deaf as well as blind. They chose their words similarly: too many adjectives, too many superlatives, too many words, too many sentences—all in their uncontrollable need to fill the void into which her absent gaze plunged them. She took advantage of their vulnerability, and behind the mask of her bright smile that had become her trademark (since she was a child Nina had always told her that her full lips and white teeth were her best asset), she would laugh at the signals sent out by these creatures in distress. She could tell by someone's footstep that his hand would be clammy. She

learned to what extent the world opens up to you if you know how to listen. She had now forgotten those early years when her eyes were open to the world. She'd felt frail only during the first few weeks after the darkness, when she could still remember what it was like to see. But years of appalling treatments had made her lose all trace of that. Since then she had garnered strength from her assumed weakness.

Mesmer was different. He had detected in her a personality as proud as it was unsettling. Above all, he could tell how much she wanted to leave the family home. That he was able to pierce this secret so easily made her impatient to be his guest, but she also worried about the power he had over her. She recalled every second of their brief encounter yet failed to locate the crack in her mask, the breach into which he could have peered in order to figure her out so well. She had brought up the subject with no one. Her parents were as much her protection as her tombstone. Her home was her haven, her wooden piano her compass. But she breathed freely only when her parents went out.

Everything about those early sighted days may have been erased from her memory, but her sense of smell clung to one thing still. Whenever she thought about that night when her gaze had been banished to the realm of darkness, the smell of amber and tobacco sprung to her mind. Her room bore the scent of her father.

Chapter 8

S HE LET THE SEASONS RUN THEIR COURSE, WAITED FOR
the winter, and chose a Friday. One day to settle in, another
to check out the place, and a third to get used to it.

This would give her three days before being alone with him,
face-to-face. Him. He in whom her father wanted to believe. He
in whom Mozart had put his trust. He whom even the Empress
had allowed to treat her.

Her father had tried to explain to her that the kind of medicine
practiced by Mesmer could in no way make her suffer. She refused
to listen to him. She could now afford to bear a real grudge toward

her father. It was official, out in the open, and she took shameless advantage of it. She felt love for this man. She was aware that she was the woman of his life, in a way her mother had probably never been, even before Maria Theresia was born.

He called her "my life's joy," and when she felt sad, which was often, she would answer, "You mean your life's sorrow." It goes without saying that he was her eyes, her anchoring. He never lost his temper or his patience with her.

He taught her the names of the colors and the trees. He had her smell the most exotic fragrances and the rarest flowers, encouraged her to taste the most unforgettable dishes. He obtained the goodwill of the Empress, brought together the city's greatest musicians.

But he broke his promise.

Since the concert at Mesmer's, she rejoiced in her newfound power to stand up to him, to have the last word, because she could brush aside his arguments, his pleas, or his anger with a turn of phrase, a terse statement. She had a few at her disposal: "You lied to me"; "You tricked me"; and the worst of all, the only one whose wounds can never heal: "You disappointed me."

You can forgive a lie, pardon some trickery. But you cannot regain what has been lost. Confidence is not a wilted plant that can be brought back to life with a bit of water. It is a highly flammable object. Doubt sets it aflame and destroys it irreparably.

"Magnetism has pierced through the night of your gaze. You will slowly be able to make out shapes. What you call shadows are in fact the contours of the objects in your midst. Can you see my arm moving?"

She opened her eyes very slowly and perceived the shadow moving up and down. She grabbed onto it, like onto a life buoy.

She recognized the scent of musk and pressed her face against it.

"Are you really going to help me see again?"

"If that is what you want, we will make it happen."

She hid her face in the hollow of his elbow.

"I'm scared."

He took her face in his hands and brought it close to his own.

"You are beautiful. You have nothing to fear."

He kissed her forehead, and she felt the quivering of his fingers against her temples. She was overwhelmed by the exquisite gentleness of his gestures.

He let go of her face abruptly, grabbed a piece of bread and placed it between her teeth. Suddenly famished, she gulped it down.

"Eat now and stop worrying. In your new life you will have to stop dissecting your every thought."

"Why? Does seeing stop you from thinking?"

He let out a short, sad laugh.

"Sight can sometimes skew our judgments. What you have in front of your eyes can blind you."

"In that case, what is the advantage of seeing?"

He thought it over before answering.

"Seeing is neither better nor worse. It is a way of discovering the reality of things and of people. You will develop your knowledge, learn to appreciate nature and to understand the human condition. Seeing can make you lucid."

"And happy?" she insisted.

He did not answer. She heard him stand up and give a maid instructions for the night. She lay down and fell asleep immediately.

Chapter 11

S HE WOKE UP IN A STATE OF GREAT CONFUSION, HER head held in place by a rough piece of cloth wrapped around her temples. She almost screamed. The thick blindfold reminded her of the cataplasms to which she had been confined as a child and which had left her with eczema for months. Then she remembered that Mesmer had mentioned protecting her eyes from the light, and she was instantly relieved. What had happened the night before was a miracle. The blackness had ceased being a homogeneous mass.

She wanted to open her eyes to try again, but the blindfold kept her eyelids tightly shut.

She called Anna, who appeared immediately by her side.

"Ah, you're there?"

"The Professor said to help you when you woke up."

"Tell him I will be ready in an hour."

"He went to Vienna to meet Madame Mesmer. They will be back in a few days. In the meantime I'm supposed to tighten your blindfold every morning and ask you not to try to open your eyes until he returns. Would you like your breakfast?"

Maria Theresia felt wounded, almost betrayed. How could he begin the treatment and then disappear?

"How will the other patients manage?"

"There are two nurses in the pavilion who tend to them as I tend to you. You're my only patient. I'll go to the kitchen and get your meal."

By habit, Maria Theresia counted Anna's footsteps as she walked away. Twenty-seven. She was hot. She pushed away the comforter. How long was "a few days"? How many hours until she would see she shadows and smell the musk? She was in a hurry to start the treatment again. No. She was not going to lie to herself. She wanted to be back in his company. She was less in a rush to get better than she was eager to be with him. She shook her head to chase away these disturbing thoughts. The blindfold was uncomfortable. It tugged at her hair. How could she miss someone she barely knew? If he managed to cure her, she didn't know how sight would affect her senses, but this impatience that took hold of her was something new.

She had learned from Nina that Madame Mesmer's face was pretty but plump and that her figure had thickened in keeping with her age. Maria Theresia hated the fact that she remembered this gossip. "I'm no better than the servants."

She spent the following days composing on the stiff piano keys a fugue that Anna described as "melancholic" and that she herself found dark, as if her tetchy mood had been translated into a disquieting, haunting tempo. She decided to call the piece "While Awaiting the Storm," because the Vienna sky was heavy and oppressive. Maria Theresia leaned her head toward the open window in hope of detecting a refreshing breeze, but none came. The city was at a standstill, on its guard. Both she and Vienna seemed to be holding their breath.

He came back with a bouquet of violets. "The same color as your moods," he said as he placed them on a pedestal table near the piano. He explained that he would remove her blindfold that evening. He preferred to wait for the sun to set, to avoid exposing her to bright light.

He started to set off to greet his other patients in the pavilion. She offered to accompany him, but he declined. His embarrassment surprised her.

"I won't be a burden, and I won't stare at anyone unbecomingly," she said mockingly. His refusal had hurt her.

"Don't underestimate yourself."

Mesmer walked away from the piano. He started pacing around the room. His footsteps seemed to mirror the progression of his thoughts.

"I have four patients there—three of them are women. They'd be jealous seeing you at my side. It would endanger their recovery."

Maria Theresia burst out laughing.

"Are they all so attached to you?"

His footsteps grew heavier, faster.

"Magnetism brings to pass a stage of intensity between the patient and the doctor. The relation I have with each of them is unique, and I want them to experience it as such."

He stopped in his tracks, staring at her back-lit profile.

"They're each about thirty years old. Your youth might disturb them."

Maria Theresia slammed the piano lid shut.

"I understand. It is best they don't cross paths with the new-comer in your harem."

The silence in the room was suddenly heavy.

"This irony is beneath you. I will see you this evening."

Chapter 12

SMARTING WITH TEARS, HER EYES WERE ON FIRE, BUT she refrained from telling him so. Once he was gone, she huddled up at the leg of the baby grand, put her arms around her knees, and rocked back and forth, just as she did as a child when the pain was too great.

So this was love? This burning-up inside? Saying the opposite of what you mean? Having your heart race in his presence and feel faint once he is gone? It was Nina's fault—Nina, who had described Mesmer as an exceptional creature; Nina, who had dwelt on his height, his intense gaze, his charisma, and the kindness of his features. Maria Theresia had been swayed by her chambermaid.

Now she is in a position to flesh out this impression of him. The heat he gives off when he approaches her; the gentleness of his hands when he clasps hers; the warmth of his breath, which, depending on the time of day, smells like coffee or mint; the volume of his voice which he can switch, as he pleases, from a booming, stentorian tone to one that is stern, cold, and unwavering, like the one he had just employed with her. But she's also known a gentle tone, which contains his emotion behind rapid breathing, almost panting.

She has never thought of a man in these terms. She feels herself blushing. She would never have described her father in terms so precise. No man has ever awakened her senses in this fashion. Mesmer is the first. Because he speaks to her as a woman, not as a blind person. He ignores her blindness. He mentions it only when discussing her treatment. This is the difference. He doesn't see her merely as Mozart's friend or the Empress's protégée; as a child prodigy spotted very early on, or a poor little rich girl plunged into darkness, or the daughter of a famous and well-connected father. Behind the social decorum and the handicap that's been wedded to her name like a preordained condition, he is interested in the person she really is: a quick-witted girl with a hunger to learn and an anxious disposition, at once distrusting everyone and desirous of trust; a budding young woman trapped in a teenage body, waiting for love to satisfy her senses and bring her fulfillment. Yes, she can admit it to herself: She dreams of having Mesmer's arms wrapped around her body, of taking shelter in that musculature, that massive manly strength.

Maria Theresia was more than in love. She had projected her every want onto Mesmer. Her need to admire, her thirst to confide, her craving to fulfill desires that she could barely comprehend. She wanted Mesmer to be a brother, a father, a friend, a confidant, a lover. She mixed together all her girlish fancies and womanly hopes and expected them all to be somehow completed by him, her doctor, her magician, her knight, her fearless savior. It sufficed simply to listen to the fugue she had composed in his house, and into which she had poured all her torments, to read her soul.

Madame Mesmer listened to it carefully, detecting in it everything one woman knows intuitively about another when both are interested in the same man. She felt pity for this vulnerable young woman of extremes. Even if she had wanted to, which was not the case, she would have been powerless to protect her. One woman's experience can never help another. In love, suffering is the only way to learn: to give in to passion body and soul, to get burnt by the flames of turmoil, incomprehension, jealousy, disappointment, bitterness—then to go off in a corner and lick your wounds, hoping to give less of yourself, and less naïvely, the next time around. Love is like Sisyphus's boulder. You hope each time you'll push it to the top of the mountain, but either it falls or it fissures. The reality of love matures young hearts. It can also destroy frail souls.

That evening he found her sitting by her bedroom window. The curtains had yet to be drawn on the moonless night, illuminated intermittently by carriage lanterns.

"You could be painted like this, wistful in the half-light. What are the street sounds telling you?"

He sat next to her on the couch. He felt drained. Between his voyage and his patients in the pavilion he had expended too much energy in too short a time.

"They speak to me of a Vienna that I do not know. A city where men dress in tailcoats, where women put on jewelry and perfume before kissing their children good night, where the theaters and opera houses are getting ready to open their doors—a city where people sing and dance, and drink up culture and wine."

"I can supply you with music, wine, and conversation," he joked as he started undoing the knots of her blindfold.

She stopped his hands with her own.

"Are you sure?"

"A doctor never stops doubting, but it is time to give it a try."

She put her hands back on her dress. He gradually loosened the blindfold.

"I am going to set your eyelids free, but do not open your eyes until I tell you to."

She smelled the rosewater that he had poured onto the compresses he used to cleanse her eyes, extremely gently, barely touching her face.

Then, nothing. Then, once again, that warm wave, a silk brush passing by her eyes without touching them.

"No pain? No burning? Turn toward me. Now open your eyelids."

The shadows were back. Less dim, less opaque. She reached out her arms toward him.

"I see . . . a shape . . . It is moving . . . I see you."

She clasped her eyes in her hands.

"It itches! My eyes are tingling!"

Mesmer leaped up, triumphant.

"This is excellent!"

He was overtaken by excitement and pride. The fatigue seemed to disappear from his body.

"This is the sign I've been waiting for. You will no longer wear a blindfold at night. Your eyes will start to breathe again and begin to be able to bear the light. Follow me with your eyes."

He moved about the room and she tried not to lose sight of him.

"It is very painful. When I move my eyes it is like having needles stuck into my skull."

Mesmer's shadow raised an arm.

"What do you see at the end of my arm?"

"I see a shadow that is less dark."

He raised the other arm.

"Ah, that spot is darker."

Mesmer laughed with delight. He shook his arms, first one, then the other. Each hand was holding a piece of cloth.

"White, black. White, black."

"White is more painful than black."

He walked back toward her and sat by her side.

"You will regain your sight. You want to. I can feel this energy in you, and thanks to it, I will be able to heal you."

He called for Anna and Madame Mesmer. They both congratulated Maria Theresia. She was given a glass of wine, which she barely touched. Her head was spinning—too much noise, too many people.

She lay down, put her hands to her eyes and then to her ears, to isolate herself a bit.

She felt like laughing and crying. She knew what would cure her, even if he didn't. It wasn't her desire to see. It was her desire to please him. This energy he felt was the love he'd inspired in her.

Chapter 13

THREE WEEKS LATER SHE HAD MADE NOTICEABLE progress, slowly getting used to the variations of light. Daylight was still too violent, but late in the afternoon and in the evening she was able to do more and more exercises; she was learning to distinguish colors, if not yet retaining their names. Gradually the headaches and the itching diminished, and the shadows became less blurry.

The hardest thing those first few weeks was to learn to work the eye muscles. Moving her eyes up and down, left and right, required an enormous effort. Her vision was still cloudy but, as she was wont to say, "I can make out more and more what's moving around in my fog."

She could increasingly discern outlines, then, still somewhat roughly, features. It was as if someone had placed thick pieces of distorting glass over her eyes.

She had a few surprises, some of them pleasant, like the sight of Mesmer's dog, a brown spaniel with long ears and sad eyes. She took a liking to it. She also loved pigeons, ducks, and all animals, generally speaking.

She had a harder time getting used to humans. It was the nose that bothered her most. It disrupted the harmony of the face. She saw it as a visible sign of a person's personality. Madame Mesmer had a small nose? "A short nose for an arid heart." Anna's was flat? Fitting for a young woman whom Maria Theresia considered "even-tempered." As for Mesmer's, straight with perfectly rounded nostrils, she decided that it was "masterful."

Maria Theresia had ambivalent feelings concerning her cure. There was the thrill of novelty, the daily discovery of a more clear-cut horizon, even if she could never fully grasp the distance separating herself from what was within her view: She could not tell the difference in distance, for example, between Mesmer's face and the hill in the window frame, and she thought them both within reach of her hand.

Nevertheless, despite the thrill of waking up every day and being able to focus more and more on the objects and landscapes in her midst, she was again thrust into a state of anxiety that she couldn't shake off. She tried to reason with herself, to account it to fatigue, because, in addition to learning to see, she had to learn the names of everything she saw. She had a hard time keeping track of this divvying up of words that seemed to her perfectly subjective and, quite honestly, nonsensical. Why a "chest of drawers" and a "wardrobe"? Why give a different word to each since both of them served the same purpose in her room? What made some words masculine and others feminine?

What discouraged her most was this newly acquired awkwardness of hers. Blind, she had always been admired for the ease with which she moved from one place to another. Now she was a clumsy creature, banging into furniture that she used to skirt around gracefully. Anna insisted that it was a matter of time, that she was too impatient, that the patients in the pavilion encountered similar difficulties getting over similar hurdles. Regardless, Maria Theresia felt diminished. Trying to assimilate all these new aspects of everyday life seemed beyond her.

Franz Anton Mesmer was infinitely patient, alternating strictness and gentleness, authority and humor. If he had an idea of the feelings she bore him, he never let it show. However, she felt that the bond uniting them was different from the usual one between doctor and patient. The results obtained and the efforts required would have justified that he allow a certain familiarity to develop. This was not the case. On the contrary. Mesmer forced upon himself a formality that betrayed an ambivalence he wanted to hide from her.

Chapter 14

ONE EVENING ON HIS WAY BACK FROM SUPPER, HE heard her crying from the entrance hall. He called Anna, who told him that Mademoiselle Paradis had blocked her door with the armchair. It was after midnight. The spaniel was whimpering in unison with her, running back and forth between the legs of his master and the rooms of his new friend.

It took a lot of persuading on Mesmer's part, but after a few long minutes he heard a piece of furniture being moved. He pushed open the door, only to come across a red face still moist with tears. Her eyes were so swollen that her gaze was inscrutable, but her demeanor left no doubt as to her utter distress.

He carried her almost all the way to her bed and sat down beside her. Her body was writhing in spasms as she wrenched her hands and dug her nails into her palms, unaware of the pain. He took her hands in his.

"What has broken your heart?"

She turned away from him without answering.

"Is it solitude that is making your suffer?"

She let out a bitter sigh but did not utter a word.

"Is the sorrow so great that even the piano in the library is of no consolation?"

She fell to his feet and started sobbing with renewed vigor. He leaned down to her, lifted her and held her in his arms as if she were a frightened child.

"What is this look of horror? What is terrifying you so much?"

She huddled against him, burying her head in his chest, shaking it left and right. He rocked her in his arms, stroking her hair. He stopped questioning her, waiting for her to calm down.

He took out a handkerchief from his pocket and gave it to her.

"There, there . . . Come now . . . Maria Theresia, you have me worried . . . Talk to me. Your sorrow is suffocating you. That's why your body is quivering. It needs oxygen. You need to say what is making you suffer. I won't tell anyone. You have my word."

This almost made her smile, but it was a hint of a smile so disillusioned that his heart sank.

"A man's word no longer means anything to me. My father didn't keep his word and here I am. I am lost, don't you see? You've destroyed something and replaced it with nothing. I'm not blind, but I cannot see. I'm living in a muddled limbo where I can't see much of anything and struggle to learn things that a three-year-old understands. I am no longer myself, but I haven't become someone else."

Her voice was getting louder, her anger more acute. She started shrieking:

"I can't play any more, do you hear me? That's what has happened, that's what is suffocating me. Yes, I'm choking with anger! I don't know how to play piano any more!"

She stood up, fueled by the rage burning inside her, out of control.

"When I sit at the keyboard, I see my hands and I freeze. My fingers have stopped obeying me. I stumble over notes. I'm off-key and imprecise! My playing is shoddy! I've lost my rhythm and my skill. Seeing has given me lead fingers! Do you hear? Lead! I didn't ask anything of anyone but everyone wants to treat me. It's the deal of the century! The stakes are high! Who wants to cure Mademoiselle Paradis? Step forward, mesdames et messieurs! Who wants a go? Does it make her ill? All the better! Cure her and you'll have fame and glory! So why worry about one little lady when the world can be yours!"

Fists clenched, she leaned over him and started pummeling him. He did not try to dodge her blows or to protect himself.

"So that's the way it is! You persuaded my father that you'd be the champion? I'm your trophy, right? You'll pin my eyes to your vest. They'll be your pride and glory! Take them! I don't want these eyes any more. Make yourself a medal, a crown. I don't want them, I don't want anything, I just want to go home to some peace and quiet. . . ."

The flow of her tears seemed never-ending. Her words became incomprehensible, incoherent. Her punches grew weaker and weaker until she wore herself out against his body, as he bore the brunt of her anger with a certain sadness.

He was sure that she would eventually regain her musical skills and resume the course of her life with no damage other than the years wasted by her blindness. He was absolutely persuaded of this. But he could see the extent of her distress, and it left him shattered.

It was the first time he'd felt anything like this. Until now he had contented himself to cure his patients without taking heed of their emotional tumult. He had treated major hysterics and egocentric neurotics whose illnesses kept them company. His patients all displayed their pain as well as their healing in a highly theatrical fashion. Convulsions, screaming, physical violence— their mental suffering lived inside them like a wild beast. They were under its influence. They couldn't fight. It drained them of their willpower.

Maria Theresia was nothing of the sort. First of all, she never played the role of victim. Being blind was part of her inherent makeup and she never seemed to question it. Some people are born with a clubfoot, protruding ears, or a hook nose. She was lacking in visual perception. But she was unaware of the ways in which she made up for it. Her perfectly oval face, her translucent complexion, her pale eyes, her silken hair, her graceful bearing in every circumstance. Then there was her elegant figure and her statuesque height. That was the first thing that had struck him the evening she came to hear him play the glass-harmonica.

Since then he had grown to appreciate her other qualities—her exceptional personality, her rare intelligence, and especially her natural poise, her frankness, a vivaciousness that distinguished her from all other girls of her background.

Maria Theresia was not trained in the game of coquetry. She knew nothing of the rules of seduction practiced in her social milieu. She never playacted, never simpered. Her mastery of her childhood misfortune made of her an old soul, lucid and intransigent, steadfast in her desire never to give in to pity or false sentiments. She was in a state of permanent alert, analyzing the intentions behind every intonation, refusing to be trapped in the role of the disabled, or even that of the patient. She put herself on the same level as whoever was speaking to her and expected that he or she do the same. Out of the question was it to inundate her with words, to make conversation—and heaven help the person who tried to cajole her with flattery. She was a responsible adult and expected to be treated as such.

For Mesmer, this kind of relationship was new. Although his other patients were older, none of them had this courage, this willpower, this hunger, this absolute need to be treated as a person. She had a very strong idea of what human relations should be. The other patients were interested only in their own mental states. Maria Theresia never indulged in any moments of elation that were in fact disguised forms of agitation. This was the other patients' forte. Mesmer admired her mental grit. He found her extraordinary in every way.

For him, physical desire was never more than the instantaneous satisfaction of a short-lived need. He now found himself for the first time truly enamored of a woman in a way that went beyond sexual attraction. He considered her his equal—impassioned, cultivated, lively, joyful. Her company was rewarding and entertaining. He treasured the time he spent with her.

The sorrow into which she had plunged was unbearable to him. He was the cause of it—he who had wanted to cure her, help her, protect her. He was responsible for her despair.

The violence of her distress triumphed over everything else: propriety, the relations he tried to maintain with his patients, the Viennese high society she came from, his marital and professional status. As if reciting his beads, he ran through his reasons for keeping her at a distance, but they inevitably caved in to the passion pulsing through him.

The punches became caresses, and the screams sighs and shouts. She let him undress her with confident abandon and welcomed him inside her as if she had been waiting her whole life for this moment, this man. Suddenly everything made sense, as if the purpose of every second of their existence was to bring them together. He knew nothing of the pleasure she discovered with him until he took her in his arms. With her he learned that the pleasure of the other was an extension of his own. For each of them it was a dazzling first time, creating between them an unalterable bond.

Chapter 15

THE DAYS THAT FOLLOWED WERE THE HAPPIEST that Maria Theresia had ever known. She felt elated and serene, taking pleasure in the present and disregarding anything that did not include him. Walking with him, seeing with him, sleeping with him, and, at night, admiring with him that illuminated horizon, the most beautiful discovery on which she had laid her eyes since she could use them: the sky dotted with stars.

Every day she made progress, getting used to the light, learning to distinguish between what was near and what was far, between what she could touch with her fingers or reach with her eyes.

Since she refused to be separated from him, he allowed her to accompany him to the pavilion. She attended his treatment sessions. She discovered the vats, the wooden tanks containing two bottles of magnetized water that were joined together by a steel rod with a moveable tip that the patients placed on the part of the body ailing them. Mesmer treated several patients simultaneously, for he was persuaded that magnetism circulated more readily in groups, with one patient holding the rod and all the patients holding hands.

Was its success grounded in science or the result of the suggestive power of its staging? Maria Theresia witnessed unforgettable scenes. Patients racked by spectacular convulsions, eyes rolled upwards, spittle drooling at the sides of the mouth, as they were ejected from their worldly shells in a spasm of extreme violence and then returned to them calm and at peace, cleansed of all woes.

She who had wanted to believe in Mesmer without trying to understand his method now learned the word "magnetism." And although she did not understand the principle or the meaning of it, she was able to take note of its effects. Perhaps the patients were hysterical, or prone to exaggeration, but no matter: After spending hours in that vat, they managed to restore a harmony between body and soul. When Mesmer told her how he tuned the limbs of the body as if they were piano strings, his words resonated with truth for her. And once he succeeded in touching and repairing every nerve, he was able to treat the mind, the erstwhile prisoner inside a tortured body.

This newfound respect for Mesmer made her love him even more. She was now a believer. She now understood why she would get better.

She imagined herself living with him, helping him treat his patients, playing piano and singing for them. She saw in the mirrors of the pavilion the image of a radiant young woman with a hearty complexion and an unbowed figure. At night she sometimes caught a glimpse of her naked body reflected in her bedroom window, and sought in that shadowy image of her body signs of the pleasure emanating from its depths within.

Chapter 16

FOR SEVERAL WEEKS SHE HAD FEARED THE VISIT. Mesmer had protected her from it for as long as he possibly could by tempering the news of her progress with advisements that her extreme melancholy justified sparing her any additional fatigue. But it was difficult to put off any longer the moment when Joseph Anton would demand that he be able to see his daughter.

One afternoon he came to her door.

Maria Theresia was terrified. She feared that her father would discover her double secret: her liaison with Mesmer and her inability to play the piano as brilliantly as she had before—no matter that she could blame everything on her frayed nerves, her moods, her difficulty to readapt to the world of sight. As for Mesmer, he was seeing a patient in the pavilion and had asked to be told if Monsieur von Paradis wished to speak with him.

"You don't look well. Too skinny."

This was the first thing the father said on seeing his daughter. The slightly plump angel he had dropped off at this house a few months earlier had shed her baby fat. And her newfound gaze had transformed her smile: It was more timid, more thoughtful; as sparkling as ever but less spontaneous. The innocent young girl was now a young woman who controlled her own feelings. She had freed herself of her father.

Joseph Anton noticed only the external signs of this transformation, and he disapproved immediately. Still, he was pleased to see how naturally she took the hat that he handed her. She led him into the house without using her hands to search for possible obstacles the way she used to do. She had some difficulty with the doorknob, which Anna, at their heels, opened for them. Yet she walked from one armchair to the other without counting her steps. They sat down.

"So, are you happy here?"

Maria Theresia had shown him into the drawing room, at the other end of the hallway that led to the library and her piano. She was dressed very simply in gray and was wearing fingerless lace gloves. She struggled to serve the tea without shaking. Anna had set out large cups so that she wouldn't spill anything. But her fluttering eyelids betrayed how nervous she was.

"I miss you, naturally, but I am happy because I can see you! And now I can make out your features. I recognize you. You're older than before, balder . . . A lot of things are coming back to me, now that I can see your face."

She paused for an instant during which Joseph Anton, uncomfortable, pretended to blow his nose.

She waited for him to look up again, then continued.

"The blackness in which I lived is finally starting to dissipate, but outlines are still fuzzy and distances hard to grasp. Still, Herr Mesmer thinks that in six to eight months things should get back to normal."

"You'll have to work faster. The Empress would like to commission Doctor von Stoerck to take note of your progress and organize a recital for the Court."

"But I need time! I spent my life blind. I have to regain certain skills before I can be expected to display them before an audience . . ."

Monsieur Paradis leaned over to his daughter.

"You must know that some of the Faculty doctors have doubts as to Mesmer's talents. They demand to see concrete results with their own eyes."

"But I'm his most recent patient. The progress I've made is still very fresh. They should visit the pavilion. The patients there are better qualified to explain the evolution of their conditions."

"They are not the Empress's protégées."

Maria Theresia stood up, shaking with indignation.

"It was your decision to send me here. It's up to you, not me, to inform those bunglers, who were never able to do anything besides torture my body, of the breakthroughs in this treatment and the progress I've made!"

She tried to move closer to her father but didn't see the cane he had placed between his legs. She tripped over it and fell, banging her head against the corner of the table. Hearing the noise, Anna sent for Doctor Mesmer.

When he came into the room, Maria Theresia was lying with her head on Anna's knees, blood dripping from her right temple.

Shaken, Monsieur Paradis rushed toward Mesmer.

"My daughter is in no state to stay by herself!"

Mesmer, very calm, greeted him respectfully.

"I didn't want to interfere in her reunion with her father."

He offered him a seat, then sat down himself.

"What do you think of Maria Theresia's progress?"

"I find her clumsy and listless."

"But you must have noticed that her eyes are open, that they are not fluttering, and that she is recovering her vision."

"I am not a doctor. Only an official report by medical professionals will allow me to judge her state."

He took his hat and gloves.

"I am aware, Herr Mesmer, of your efforts to treat my daughter. But understand that a more . . . objective opinion would put me entirely at ease. "

Mesmer concurred.

"I am at the disposal of my colleagues."

Monsieur Paradis gave him his hand.

"Very well. Many of them will agree to your invitation. I am pleased to be able to extend it to them."

He started walking to the door and indicated to Mesmer that he need not follow.

"I'll see myself out."

He looked in his daughter's direction.

"Take care of her. And tell her that my wife sends all the love a mother feels for a daughter."

Mesmer gestured to Anna that she see him to the door.

His heavy footsteps made the floorboards squeak and the spaniel bark.

He was gone.

Immediately, no longer able to control herself, Maria Theresia burst into tears in Mesmer's arms.

"I hate them all! You can't let them examine me. I won't let them touch me!"

Mesmer stroked her hair sadly.

"I promise they won't do a thing to you. But you cannot avoid answering their questions. We'll prepare for them. You'll pass their tests with flying colors!"

She held on to him.

"How will I play the piano?"

Mesmer looked at her tenderly.

"It is just a question of time."

"But the Empress seems very eager to hear me play. And the Empress is not to be kept waiting."

Mesmer held her against him.

"We'll invent a contagious disease for you. No one will dare come see you . . . Except for me."

His burst of laughter managed to reassure her. But he was worried. Joseph Anton was ill-disposed toward him. Mesmer detected a certain jealousy that would undermine the sympathy Paradis had shown him until now. He feared that the father's feelings might make him turn a blind eye to reason. From now on, Mesmer's career would depend on the performance of his famous patient.

Chapter 17

THE TRAINING TO WHICH MESMER SUBJECTED HER WAS equal to that of a professional athlete. He watched over the quality of her sleep and regulated the rest for her eyes. He prevented her from playing the piano so that she would not be overtaken by melancholy. He selected various objects, the names of which she knew and which she could easily identify, to place in the large drawing room where he planned to invite his colleagues. He had her memorize the names of certain colors and match them to corresponding words. He made sure that the same colors figured significantly in the room, in the hue of a curtain, a book, a bouquet of flowers, or a brooch pinned to her dress. He also made sure to position the curtains so the drawing room would not be too bright, for daylight sometimes gave her headaches. He walked with her in the garden to make her complexion hearty. He was in a state of constant tension as he awaited, day after day, his colleagues' arrival.

These preparations justified the time he devoted to Mademoiselle Paradis. Madame Mesmer had decided to spend the winter with relatives in London, so he and his patient no longer had to hide from anyone except the staff—though Anna was nobody's fool.

Maria Theresia was less anxious. Mesmer's daily presence was magical, stimulating. Perfectly self-assured for the first time ever, she felt only contempt for her future visitors. She was ready to receive them and to submit to their examinations and interrogations.

Her only fear was no longer being able to play the piano. The dread was such that for the time being she preferred not to go near a keyboard. "Afterwards," she said. "We'll see afterwards." This "afterwards" comprised everything that she preferred not to think about: the piano, her parents, her absolute refusal to live with them again, her terror of no longer being able to live with Mesmer. Afterwards was the future, which she did not trust at all. The present fulfilled her. For the first time in her life, she had found her place in the world.

Chapter 18

THE FIRST PERSON TO COME TO EVALUATE MARIA Theresia's progress was a Court doctor, Herman de Ost. Mesmer, who considered Ost a friend, was enormously relieved. They had an amicable relationship. Professor de Ost had always encouraged Mesmer to continue his research for a new kind of medicine.

Ost spent two hours with Maria Theresia. He was charmed by her enthusiasm and admired her ability to distinguish between objects. He left convinced of her progress.

"Although I cannot say that her vision is excellent, I am certain that she is no longer blind and recommend wholeheartedly that she continue being treated by Professor Mesmer."

Such was the wording of his report, the optimism of which was not well received by Professor Barth, the famous oculist specializing in cataract operations. He had asserted in the past to the Empress that her protégée was incurable and did not wish to be proved wrong. He decided to judge for himself the legitimacy of these claims.

Gustav Barth, accompanied by a colleague, arrived at Mesmer's home late one morning. He greeted the master of the house rather coldly and refused to meet with the young woman in the drawing room into which he had been shown.

"Ost examined her inside. I wish to do so in broad daylight."

Maria Theresia was thus asked to sit on a stone bench in the sun.

She immediately began blinking, of which Barth made much ado.

"None of my cataract patients has ever had a problem with the noonday sun!"

Mesmer objected that cataract patients were not blind and that their optical nerves never suffered any damage. Their vision was impaired for a few months, not for years, as was the case with Maria Theresia.

Barth commanded him to leave them alone.

"Who knows the power of your magnetism? I wouldn't want to take the risk of letting it interfere with our examination!"

Mesmer had no other choice but to obey. He went back into the house, expecting the worst.

He was furious, powerless to protect her from this inauspicious visit. Maria Theresia was not used to being assailed by a slew of questions from malevolent strangers. She was sitting in the sun; she had not had lunch. She was alone, and the panic she was feeling would make her answers incoherent.

But Mesmer underestimated his mistress's determination to meet the challenge. It was Barth who had confined her head to a cataplasm for months on end. She intended to make him regret his judgments.

"What do you see at the other end of the garden, on your left?"

"A long, pale blue ribbon that is in fact a river. The Danube."

"What is the sky like today?"

"Deep blue, as it often is in Vienna during the winter. It is called a dry cold."

"What word do you use to describe that thing reaching up to the sky?"

"A tree. A holm oak, to be exact. Down the path, by the lake, are some rosebushes."

"What color is your dress?"

"Sea green, like my eyes. My favorite."

"And the ring I'm wearing?"

"A ruby, I think. Bloodred."

"What am I holding?"

"A white handkerchief."

"Yes, but apparently you do not see the yellow border around it."

"I recognize the object."

"Yes, but your description is imprecise."

Maria Theresia started to feel the onslaught of fatigue pressing against her temples.

"What do you see in the palm of my hand?"

"I see nothing. The object in your hands is reflecting sunlight onto me. It is very unpleasant."

She was forced to use her hand to protect her eyes from the reverberation that sent needles into her skull and made her vision blur.

"It's a mirror! Every woman knows a mirror!"

"My eyesight is too recent for me to have acquired a taste for coquettishness."

She was hot. Her head was spinning. She felt nauseous.

"What is Professor Umlauer holding in his hand?"

Everything around her was blurred.

"A stick?"

He let out a smug laugh.

"A cane, you mean. What color is it?"

"Dark, I think."

"Black! Not a very difficult color to recognize!"

"I know. I've lived in blackness since I was a child . . ."

"And what is this?"

He held out a round, thick object. She could not even make out its color.

"A candle?"

"Come now! Think! Do doctors walk around with candles in their pockets? It's a cigar, like the ones Mesmer loves to smoke!"

"He never smokes in front of me for fear of irritating my eyes."

She closed her eyes, tilted her head backwards, and started when suddenly he took her hand and placed it on his coat collar.

"What do you feel beneath your fingers?"

"You're hurting me. Feels like dog hair!"

Barth stood up, revolted.

"It's ermine!"

Mesmer, who had been watching from a window, stormed into the garden to put an end to an interview that was visibly exhausting his patient.

Barth walked toward him.

"This young woman may not be blind, but she has a hard time describing a view that she has had several months to study. She had trouble distinguishing the objects we submitted to her. And sunlight makes her feel ill. I fear that without your daily efforts she would once again be engulfed by the blackness she once knew. I admit that progress has been made, but

I cannot state for a fact that Mademoiselle Paradis has regained her sight."

Mesmer had a hard time containing his anger.

"In that case I myself will present her to the Empress, who will no doubt be less loath to acknowledge that progress has been made."

"The Empress placed her trust in me a long while ago. Mark my words, such an audience will never happen. By the way, might I ask Mademoiselle Paradis to play one of her compositions for us? I am curious to see how her newfound eyesight has affected her playing. The Empress is a huge admirer of her pianistic skills. In fact, it just crossed my mind: If, thanks to your care, Mademoiselle Paradis ceases being blind, would not her father have to give up the annuity of two hundred ducats?"

He leaned toward Maria Theresia.

"Do you really wish that I declare you cured? You should think it over."

Beside himself, Mesmer grabbed Maria Theresia by the arm.

"Mademoiselle Paradis needs to rest after the exhausting examination you have submitted her to. I will not see you to your carriage. Understand that my first priority is her health."

He headed up the front steps, pulling Maria Theresia hastily in his tow, to get her out of sight before she lost consciousness.

Barth shot a knowing glance at Umlauer.

They had won this round.

Chapter 19

MARIA THERESIA KEPT TO HER ROOM FOR SEVERAL days. Was it the glare of daylight or the fragility of her nerves? She lost some of her eyesight; plunging back into a world of shadows, she asserted that everything around her was a blur and that she could no longer distinguish objects and colors.

She started playing piano again, set on regaining her agility. She played with a blindfold so as not to be tempted to look at her fingers on the keyboard.

In truth, she was lost.

Mesmer had saved her from a life divided between the authority of her parents and the demanding routine of concerts. But nowadays her progress caused more trouble than her blindness ever had, and she no longer knew what was preferable: to be blind or to give up trying to regain her sight. In either case, she ran the risk of being sent back to her parents' home. So she opted for this no man's land, a semblance of sight, enough to keep up the treatment yet not enough to be declared cured. Alone, she walked about the house and garden, but she refused all attempts to work on her eyes.

She managed to have the rumor spread in Vienna that Barth's examination had increased her melancholia and worsened her eyes. She was hoping both to hurt him and gain herself some time.

Mesmer was no dupe, but he did not try to gainsay her, even though he was furious not to be able to parade his triumph for the world to see. He had cured Mademoiselle von Paradis, and the four patients in the pavilion were recovering from their nervous disorders. But how could he persuade his colleagues that simply by placing his hands on receptive bodies he could obtain better results than the treatments they recommended? How could he persuade such self-satisfied gentlemen? Why had he ceased being respected as a doctor the minute he'd started getting concrete results?

Mademoiselle Paradis's case awakened his old complexes about his inferior social class and his all-consuming need for social recognition. He had thought that treating her would be the crowning achievement of his career. Now he understood that it might in fact be his downfall. He could, without anyone second-guessing him, obtain satisfactory results on weaker minds or members of the lower classes. But succeeding where his illustrious colleagues had failed, on someone they had been unable to treat—this was unacceptable. By taking up interest in her, he had overreached himself. He was accepted as an original, an eccentric, a patron of the arts doubling as a man of science who afforded himself the luxury of exploring the fringes of medicine. But not as a scientist revolutionizing his era.

It became apparent that his peers were refusing to associate with him. The Court doctors snubbed him. Even the Baron von Stoerck, his mentor and supporter, avoided crossing paths with him and spoke of him to colleagues with references to his "imagination." Fewer people came to his parties. They invited him less to their own. He was no longer in the uppermost stratum of high society.

He decided to restore his reputation. He was seen, with Madame Mesmer at his side, at every concert, every opera. In his home he welcomed illustrious musicians, singers, and dancers. He held sumptuous banquets. Mademoiselle von Paradis was no longer anywhere to be seen. She was kept out of the Mesmers' social picture. Her poor health, after all, placed such festivities off-limits to her.

Mesmer beat her at her own game.

He spent less time with her during the day. At night he visited her less often. He was still enamored of her youth, fascinated by her innocent yet lucid state of mind. He was still convinced that he could wrench her from her shadows, but with his own future now at stake, he was less sure that he wanted devote all his energy to her recovery.

"I am no longer your favorite patient," sighed Maria Theresia when they were alone together in her room.

Mesmer protested her use of irony.

"You govern my thoughts and my future lies in your hands."

"This is what I deplore! Why must I offer proof of my recovery when it is still incomplete? I would be better off in the pavilion with your anonymous patients. At least no one comes to monitor their health!"

"I informed your father of the reason for your relapse. I also told him that you have started making progress again but that it is too soon to plan a concert."

"The Empress has to see the progress I've made so that you can take credit for it and I can be spared further torment. If I ask her for an audience, she cannot refuse, can she?"

She was sitting at her writing desk. Mesmer turned his back to her, too moved to confront her.

She stood up and came beside him at the window, putting her arm in his, staring at the sky.

"I don't see any light, not even the moon. Does it mean there is

bad weather coming tomorrow . . . or have we fallen from grace?
Is our lucky star no longer shining on us?"

Mesmer was on the verge of tears. He took her hands, held
her against him.

"I wanted to protect you, but I cannot keep any secrets from
you. We're going to have to fight. A rumor has spread through
Vienna that is sullying your reputation as well as mine. People
are saying that we are lovers and that your so-called progress is
the effect of 'amorous suggestion,' that is, some power I purport-
edly have over you. In other words, in my presence you can see
things that you wouldn't be able to see alone. Something along
the lines of the sorcerer and his willing victim. They say our
work is a hoax."

She let him pull her closer.

"So our love is no more than a premeditated power play on
your behalf? An attempt to manipulate me? That in addition
to being blind, I am stupid and impressionable? You are well-
versed in the rules of high society—tell me how to fight against
an enemy who has no face."

"Your father hinted that if you went home, it would put an
end to the gossip."

She clutched onto him, begging him, abandoning all
restraint.

"I don't want to. I can't. I can no longer live without you.
My father rules over his house with an iron hand. He terrorizes
everyone. He loves me, but he keeps me under his thumb, in a

way you would never do, even out of love! If the gossipmongers knew what life was like in the Paradis home, my father would have been stripped of his privileges long ago!"

"That is exactly the other rumor being spread. If you get better, your father will be deprived of the generous annuity the Empress allotted you."

Maria Theresia laughed bitterly.

"There we go! Barth's threat is finally being acted out! So let him be deprived of that annuity! Why should money be worth more than my health? My father will not let such rumors be spread because he is the first person sullied by them."

"Think again! He is terrified at the idea of losing this godsend that has changed your lives for fifteen years now. The taste for this manna is very easy to acquire and very hard to lose. He will never give up his two hundred gold ducats."

Maria Theresia slid onto the bed and buried her head in the pillows.

"Cursed! I am cursed! My blindness made them suffer and my recovery has made them mad. Even you prefer me ill to cured. Life is so cruel! It allows me to discover passion and harmony, then steals it away as if it were a mirage! What good is seeing if all it does is open your eyes to the truth of human nature? Have I been through all this just to come eye to eye with cowardice, lies, and trickery? To see you run away from me because I've become a burden? It is better to die than to be confronted with greedy, wicked men incapable of love!"

She was screaming, banging her head and beating her chest. She let him subdue her, then she collapsed, howling her turmoil.

Mesmer held her against him, ashamed. He knew her words rang true.

She had asked for nothing. She had listened to the doctors, to her father, and now to Mesmer. They had all betrayed her trust.

His sincerity was beyond reproach. But feelings evolve quickly. Depending on circumstances, what was true one minute may no longer be true the next.

Now he was ready to forgo Maria Theresia in order to save his career.

Chapter 20

MARIA THERESIA THREW HERSELF INTO HER exercises at the piano. She had removed her blindfold and was rehearsing tirelessly the same movement, a Mozart adagio. Losing her temper, she would rail aloud against her fingers when they hesitated at the keyboard or hit two keys instead of one. She couldn't separate her eyes from her hands when she was playing; if she was not intrigued by her short fingernails as she struck the black and white keys, she was distracted by the light reflecting off the piano's polish. She forced herself to act blind by keeping her eyes off the piano and staring at a point in the distance, near the window with its curtains drawn.

She was determined to regain control of the keyboard so as to be able to play for the Empress. She wanted to prove that her talent was intact even if the added allure of her blindness had been lost. She wanted to continue receiving the annuity, not as compensation for a handicap but to make up for the years she had invested in trying to become a world-renowned virtuoso.

Having fully recovered the sight that Barth's examination had put in jeopardy, she had come to the conclusion that her progress remained extremely fragile because the slightest agitation could send her back into the world of shadows. Informed that her mother wanted to visit her, Maria Theresia responded that the emotions provoked by such a meeting would be harmful to her health. In truth, she had no desire to be confronted with the discomposure of this woman for whom she felt little affection. She had no recollection whatsoever of any tenderness she'd received from a mother who was so decidedly not maternal.

So, when Anna knocked at her door to tell her that she had a visitor in the drawing room, Maria Theresia refused to go, complaining that she had been interrupted in her work and could not be seen in her dressing gown with her face red and her hair uncombed. Rather than giving in to her refusal, however, Anna insisted, arguing that Mademoiselle would be very happy indeed to meet the person awaiting her.

Anna shifted from foot to foot, trying to convince her, when all of a sudden Maria Theresia heard a footstep that made her bolt from the piano stool, rush to the door, and run open-armed into the familiar scent of starch that characterized the refuge of her childhood. Nina laughed joyously, spinning her in her arms as she had when Maria Theresia was a child. The two of them shed tears, kissed, pulled back to contemplate each other's faces, and then fell back into each other's arms, their embrace magical.

"Your eyes are lighter. They are pale green now!" marveled the servant.

"Nina . . . Here you are . . ."

Overwhelmed, Maria Theresia touched Nina's curly hair, her round cheeks, her cool, callused hands, as if she were getting her bearings.

"How is Runter? Remember how you hid him under your apron? You put ribbons in my hair. I would fidget just to annoy you. I'd get money for every knot that came undone."

"And the rabbit game. Do you still remember it?"

"Clever rabbit, hide from my eyes, but I the cat shall thee surprise!" answered Maria Theresia breathlessly, recalling the nursery rhyme from before the shadow days.

After the memories, the hugging, the confidences, the tears, after having partaken of the snack that Anna had prepared for them, they went out for a walk.

Maria Theresia walked lazily, relieved to feel Nina's arm firmly round her waist. She leaned against her like a fledgling who had flown too far away and at last rediscovered the security of the nest. She had confided in no one for months and was happy to be able to tell Nina of her liaison with Mesmer, her initial elation, and her present anxiety.

"My father hasn't sent you, I hope?" she asked, worried that her greatest ally had switched sides.

"He doesn't know that I am here. He thinks I've gone to see my family for a few days."

"You have brothers and sisters and cousins! How lucky! I have only my parents. A mother who lives in the shadow of her husband and a tyrannical father who decides my every move."

"It is thanks to your father that Herr Mesmer is treating you."

"Yes, but between the prospect of losing my annuity if I am cured and ruining my reputation by staying here, he must have serious regrets!"

She spoke with an ironic smile that Nina had never before seen.

"Yes, Nina, here I have learned cynicism and bitterness, two feelings that were foreign to me. For a long time my blindness protected me from a reality that is not pretty to behold. What I have discovered scares me much more than the shadows that surrounded me. I have opened my eyes to a world that I knew nothing of, and it grows more and more disappointing every day. There is no room in it for simple, naïve souls who think that happiness is all about loving others. You can't get by on love, or art. Ambition is the force that drives this world. People care more about clawing their way to fame and manipulating others than they do about what makes a concerto work."

She took Nina's hands in her own.

"I can admit it to you: I am having difficulty playing the piano because I have to learn to stop staring at the keyboard. But this is not the only reason. I have lost the faith I had in music. I used to think it would help me express emotions that an audience could share with me. During a concert the listeners and I would engage in a sort of conversation. There was an exchange between what I gave them and the way they received it. Their listening returned to me my emotion a hundredfold. Well, I no longer believe that. People listen and they are probably moved, but their attention is distracted by what's running through their minds, and now I fear that they send back to me nothing other than their own vanity. They have no time to be affected by the music, even though music alone has the power to raise their hearts and ease their minds. They cannot be bothered. This is what preoccupies me now when I play. I analyze the world coldly. I no longer idealize it. As I've lost my conviction in my talent, I can't convince anyone with my talent. This is what I've become, Nina. A girl without illusions. Music has ceased being my dream world. Now that I see the real world, I live with nightmares."

Exhausted by having opened her heart to Nina, Maria Theresia suggested they head back to the house. They walked in silence, arm in arm, closer to each other than ever before.

As they entered through the French windows in the back of the house, they heard a commotion in the entrance hall. They rushed to see what was going on, only to discover Anna and the butler face-to-face with Monsieur and Madame von Paradis, the two of them screaming, demanding to see Herr Mesmer at once.

They saw their daughter and hurried toward her, not even noticing Nina at her side. Instead of taking her in her arms, her mother, in a state of extreme agitation, shook Maria Theresia violently.

"Hurry, gather some things. We'll send someone later for the rest. You're coming with us!"

Joseph Anton was still arguing with the butler. They could hear Mesmer in the garden, furious that her parents had entered his home unannounced.

He reached the front door and asked Anna to explain the situation.

Monsieur Paradis stormed toward him.

"I order you to return my daughter to me!"

Mesmer bowed, too ceremoniously to be paying his respects. As was his wont, he responded to excess with calm and to agitation with utter self-control.

"Mademoiselle Paradis is here because you have done me the honor of allowing me to cure her. You can take her back whenever you want."

"I want her to leave with us immediately."

Mesmer turned to Maria Theresia. She looked at him scathingly.

He gave her an imperceptible nod, then spoke to her father.

"You do agree with me that it is up to her to decide."

"My daughter will do what I order her to do."

"Never!"

The shout escaped her mouth to the stupefaction of everyone present—a shout so desperate that Joseph Anton stopped in his tracks, stunned to hear such a cry of distress coming from his daughter.

His wife, however, was so offended by this lack of respect that she took three steps toward her daughter and slapped her once on each cheek, shouting:

"We sacrificed everything for you. You shall do as you are told!"

She shook her, beat her. She was out of control, letting out years of bottled-up rage.

Maria Theresia protected her face, crying, while Mesmer and Nina tried to wrench her from her mother's grip.

When she finally stood up, she shrieked:

"I don't see anything any more!"

She put her hands to her eyes, took a few wavering steps toward Mesmer, and then lost consciousness.

Chapter 21

A FEW HOURS LATER, SHE WAS LYING FEVERISH IN HER bed, tossing her head in every direction, murmuring incomprehensibly. Her face was extremely pale, her body heaving as if waves of pain were coursing in spasms through her.

Nina tried to apply cool compresses to her forehead, while Mesmer massaged her temples with camphor oil.

Mesmer stood up, leaned over her bed, removed the cover, and placed his hands on her ankles. For a long moment he hovered over her without moving, before he drew closer without touching her further. Then, slowly, he worked his hands up the length of her body until he reached her head. Then he did so again and again, repeatedly increasing the tempo of his hands.

Suddenly, Maria Theresia stiffened. Her limbs tensed. She held her breath for several seconds. Mesmer removed his hands, and immediately her body relaxed. She started breathing normally again; her face slackened. Her sleep became peaceful.

Nina watched Mesmer admiringly. When they were sure that she'd fallen into a deep sleep, they walked to the window.

The full moon illuminated the garden. The night had washed away the trauma of the day.

"That was an epileptic fit, wasn't it, Doctor?" Nina was over-wrought, panicking at having seen her dear mistress go from painful lucidity to sheer confusion.

"I'm afraid so. She will need time to recover, but I doubt we'll be given any."

Nina stared at him, shocked.

"Isn't it the doctor who decides what is best for his patient?"

He placed his hands on her shoulders to reassure her.

"I can only suggest. I have no real authority. Between her father and the Court doctors, who knows what may happen?"

Nina insisted.

"But aren't you going to protect her?"

Mesmer stared out the window, lost in his thoughts.

He took a moment to answer, and when he did he seemed far away, as if speaking to himself.

"I'd like to have devoted my life to treating her, to showing her the world. I'd have made of her an exceptional artist. I think I would have made her happy. But life has decided otherwise. My colleagues want my ruin. Monsieur Paradis wants his daughter. Their schemes will destroy her health, my career, and our future."

He was overtaken by a wave of fatigue. He closed his eyes, then stood up straight and warmly clasped Nina's hands in his own.

"I will try to keep her here as long as possible, but I am not optimistic. You are more than welcome to stay here as well."

Maria Theresia was fast asleep. He stroked her cheek, then headed for the door.

"Good night, Nina. Thank you for watching over her. Later, when she has doubts about me, you will tell her that I loved her."

The door closed silently behind him.

Chapter 22

THE NEWS MADE ITS WAY QUICKLY TO THE COURT. Joseph Anton von Paradis never tired of recounting his misfortunes. It became his mission to broadcast how Mesmer's treatment had ruined his daughter's constitution. He appeared not to see how such reports might confirm the rumor of the liaison between the two.

He dared not consult the Empress. Instead, he left his daughter's fate in the hands of Professor von Stoerck. The head doctor to the Court was only too happy to take action against the faddish practitioner whose methods were not recognized by the official medical community, whose craft Stoerck himself had practiced and whose principles he'd defended.

He immediately contacted Cardinal Migazzi, president of the Commission of Morality, who in turn sent Mesmer a letter, demanding in the name of the Empress that he desist in his "trickery." So as not to be seen taking too extremist a view against a treatment that certain colleagues still praised, however, he specified that Maria Theresia's parents could reclaim their daughter only once it was ascertained that her return home would constitute no danger to her health.

The hypocrisy of the letter was obvious. As president of the Austrian medical community, Migazzi was destroying Mesmer's career without demonstrating that his treatment was in any way harmful. And he left to the parents the responsibility for a decision the consequences of which they alone would know or suffer.

"How can I damage the eyes of a patient whose optical nerve, according to everyone who has examined her, is perfectly intact? Her father has noticed a change in her nervous disposition, but his child recovered her sight after fifteen years of blindness. Is not a spell of melancholia perfectly comprehensible? Why does the Commission refuse to pay heed to the colleagues who have attested to the evolution of her ability to distinguish people and objects, shadows and light?"

Mesmer wore himself out sending letters to von Stoerck, who never answered and refused to meet with him.

The term of the official letter forced Joseph Anton von Paradis to allow some time to pass before his next visit to Mesmer's house.

The violence on the occasion of his last visit, all the more traumatic because it seemed to spring up out of nowhere, had left Maria Theresia blind once again. It would take Mesmer more than a month to again retrieve her sight.

The melancholy of these final weeks spent in Mesmer's care should have been painful for Maria Theresia, yet she seemed more at peace than she had for some while. She had stopped living in fear of the future because it now seemed to be inarguably fixed. She embraced each day with a newfound serenity. Her exceptional calm surprised Nina, who was used to her mistress's extreme—and extremely unpredictable—mood swings. Maria Theresia explained her state of mind in a cryptic manner that, far from reassuring Nina, alarmed her even more.

"I know now what meaning I must give to the rest of my existence."

When Nina shared her concern with Mesmer, he admitted to being as nonplussed as she.

Maria Theresia knew that in a few days she would be forced to leave this house where she had discovered, in the course of several months, feelings that can take a woman a lifetime to understand and accept: the gift of oneself, sharing, passion and its transformation into a less voracious tenderness comprised of kindness and a different way of sharing. She had discovered the perversities of the soul. Toward her parents she felt remote feelings of love and filial duty. She had given herself body and soul to a man whose reputation in the country had been shattered. Her newly recovered eyesight brought into focus how disappointing reality truly was.

Nevertheless, she was smiling, and even humming. She took endless walks in the garden. She knew its every path, every stone bench. In the pavilion, where she would participate in the magnetism sessions, her new confidence spread to the few patients still residing there despite the malicious rumors as to their famous doctor's methods.

She had given up playing piano without the blindfold. She herself now tied it around the eyelids and practiced for hours on end with her eyes shut in their prison.

Mesmer listened to her without her knowing, troubled by this new ardor in her playing. He detected a sort of self-assurance, an independence that he had not noticed before. It was as if she had set herself free of him, had swept away her fears, and was preparing to confront her future with equanimity. "She is ready," thought Mesmer as he listened to her interpret her own compositions or those of her favorite musicians with an authority he had never before noticed. He felt that she had made a decision—but to do what? This temerity with no apparent purpose scared him.

They still spent long nights together. She never tired of staring at the sky, asking him to repeat the names of the stars and planets.

She had countless questions about the moon and sun, and always made sure that she could situate the east, west, north, and south. One day she asked Anna to show her the difference between beige and gray. Anna brought her two cushions and Maria Theresia spent a long time comparing them.

Her gestures grew less spontaneous. She gave the impression that she was constantly thinking, filling her brain with annotations the importance of which only she knew. She learned the names of her favorite flowers, the components of certain perfumes, and even the ingredients necessary to make the desserts she liked best. She spent long stretches of time stroking the spaniel and whispering her secrets to him.

Sometimes she sought solace in Nina's arms.

"I'm filling up my memory," she would say jokingly.

"Why do you?" a worried Nina would ask. "Are you afraid you'll forget this house?"

Maria Theresia would then cast a knowing smile and, as if speaking to herself, say:

"My stay here is etched in me. No one will never erase these memories."

Chapter 23

IT WAS A WEDNESDAY. THE GARDEN SMELLED OF FRESHLY cut grass. Birds were chirping and the sun was heating up the stone benches. Her parents were expected before lunch. Officially, they were taking her to get some fresh air in the country. It had been agreed that she would return to the house on Landstrasse to resume her treatment, although no future date had been set.

Nina had locked the trunks. Anna had made a bouquet of flowers from the garden.

Maria Theresia returned the piano key to its owner, refusing his offer that she keep it as a souvenir. She tried to make light of it.

"When you play this piano, you will fancy you are seeing me."

He countered her seeming lightness with serious advice.

"Watch out for your nerves. I have left instructions to Nina—"

She cut him off.

"We will never meet again. You know that as well as I. My stay here has been an invaluable learning experience. Thanks to you, I know who I am and what I can expect from life. I've taken my future in my own hands. What will happen to me must not worry you. Some will see the mark of fate or destiny . . . no matter! You have cured me. I know it. Don't ever doubt it."

He wanted to draw her toward him, but she pulled away from his grasp.

"I am returning you to your wife and patients. I know that my presence here has ruined your reputation. I am sorry. Ultimately, both of us will bear traces of this adventure. As for me, I've decided to regret nothing."

The butler came to announce Monsieur von Paradis's arrival. He then escorted Mesmer and his patient to the front steps.

They bid each other farewell in public, under the teary eyes of Anna and Nina.

Madame von Paradis had not made the trip.

Ill at ease, Joseph Anton tried to persuade Mesmer to accept the velvet purse he was holding out to him.

"It's only fair to compensate you for the care you gave her and for the staff you employed."

Mesmer repeated that the cure, undertaken at his own initiative, would remain free of charge and that no contract, not even a verbal one, should ever be changed after the fact.

"I consider that I have fulfilled my mission, albeit imperfectly, because the patient requires another six months' care."

"We'll see to it!" said old Paradis half-heartedly, glancing at his coachman, in a rush to get this over with.

"Take care, Maria Theresia."

Mesmer bowed solemnly toward her, clasping her hand a moment too long.

"I will never forget you," she whispered.

The snap of a whip, the banging of hoofs, the carriage in the distance.

On June 8, 1777, a glorious summer day, Mademoiselle Paradis left the home of Franz Anton Mesmer for good.

Chapter 24

MONSIEUR PARADIS MOVED HIS DAUGHTER TO THE Bavarian countryside, which at this time of year offered a luxurious palette of yellows and greens. One of his obligors had lent him a property. It was vast and comfortable.

Maria Theresia told her father that Nina alone would tend to her. Mesmer had entrusted the chambermaid with lotions and ointments, as well as some know-how. Maria Theresia was allowed to occupy the children's guesthouse in the middle of the garden. It became her territory. She had a piano brought in, and she lived there with Nina.

Her reunion with her mother was civil. Maria Theresia vowed not to hold a grudge since their last meeting, and her mother responded with hugging and kissing, all the requisite outpourings and effusions.

Maria Theresia was perfectly amicable, but her behavior was devoid of affection. She had decided to maintain a certain harmony in the family and acted accordingly. Nina sensed quite rightly that this was her mistress's way of negotiating her independence. She played the role of the perfect daughter; it was she who set the rules, however. Her parents felt too guilty to try to recast the situation in their favor. In their eyes, they had flawlessly extricated themselves from the deadlock with Mesmer. Their daughter was back, her honor saved and her annuity guaranteed—so said the Empress, relieved that the scandal was behind them all.

The day after she moved into the guesthouse, Maria Theresia, claiming that the journey had exhausted her, stayed in bed and refused to see anyone. She even forbade Nina to enter her room, requesting that she leave her meals at the door. She explained that she did not feel strong enough to undergo the slightest treatment. She wanted to sleep and accustom herself to being alone once again.

For over a week no one saw her. She closed the shutters in her bedroom and pulled the curtains in the drawing room, where she played piano every day.

After nine days Nina was so worried that she disobeyed her

mistress's orders and entered her bedroom with her meal on a tray.

Surprised by the noise, Maria Theresia, who had been sitting looking out the window, turned around. Horrified, Nina put her hands to her mouth, dropping the tray to the floor without even noticing. Maria Theresia's eyes were purple and swollen, the lids burnt by the sun, the skin parched. Her face was beet red.

Nina rushed to pull her chair out of the sunlight. Maria Theresia let out an amused sigh.

"Are you frightened the sun will harm my eyes? It is too late. The damage is done. I put saltwater compresses on my eyes. I did everything I was told not to do for the past six months. Don't start blaming me. The decision is mine."

Nina burst into tears, horrified at what her mistress was hinting at.

"You're harming your eyes? Why do you want to hurt yourself?"

"Ah, dear Nina, you're mistaken. It's the opposite. I am putting an end to my suffering."

"I don't understand what you're telling me."

Maria Theresia took her by the hand. Her voice grew softer.

"You understand perfectly well, even if it bothers you. I refuse to become a circus freak. I feel I'm part angel, part demon. I used to be a virtuoso. Now I play less well than the most mediocre concert artist. I used to be blind. Now I can see if I'm in a shaded, quiet place surrounded by kind people—which limits my capabilities.

"I loved a man passionately. He had feelings for me, but he sacrificed me to his career. He offered me the dream of a shared life and then let others destroy that dream. Seeing is a pleasant sensation, but opening my eyes to the truth of the human heart is a spectacle I'd rather forget. Man is more attractive when he is left to the imagination. I've seen enough. Instead of living among liars, flatterers, and careerists, I prefer my own world. The one in which each color has its note and each chord its truth. The one in which I am mistress of my own destiny.

"Blind people inspire fear. If they're talented, this fear turns into respect. This is fine with me. Again mastering my piano is my priority. As I am now losing the last bit of sight left to me, I will soon have regained my skill. The technique will follow. Every day I see less and I play better. Most of all, I have faith. Girls who love Christ become nuns. I love music so much that I will dedicate my life to it. Sight impaired my playing. I give it up with no regrets. It has brought me pipe dreams, no more."

Nina nodded pensively.

"You intend to become a blind virtuoso, if I understand correctly. But afterwards, what about your future?"

Maria Theresia opened her arms theatrically.

"Travel! I have decided to travel the world. I want to play and sing wherever I am invited. Don't you see that a world without music is blind? Music is the language of the soul. I want to devote myself to it, so the world will listen to it rather than simply hear it."

"How will you go about this? You cannot travel by yourself. Voyages are long and costly adventures . . ."

"Soon it will be within my means. The annuity that my father started receiving when I turned five will revert to me once I am eighteen. I will see to it."

She put her hands on her chambermaid's shoulders.

"I have a proposal for you. If I am able to travel, will you be willing to accompany me, to be my eye, my confidante, my memory?"

She lay her head next to Nina's.

"Forgive me for having withdrawn into silence. I needed to find my way once again. Now I know my calling. I will keep no more secrets from you."

The news took two months to reach the capital. Mademoiselle Paradis had totally lost her sight. Joseph Anton explained that his daughter's state had deteriorated day by day and that her condition was now irreversible.

Critics of magnetism took this as the final proof of what they had always considered a hoax. Rumor had it that Mesmer's powers were some form of bewitchment. During the weeks that followed, the pavilion patients had returned home. Those who were well hid their health for fear that people would say they were victims of witchcraft.

The faddish doctor, patron of the arts, and charismatic gentleman, was now cursed and reviled. Von Stoerck intended to have him deported from Austria as an "Undesirable Foreigner."

He'd need not go to this extreme.

In the winter of 1777, one year after having treated Mademoiselle Paradis, Mesmer, forsaken by all, left Vienna for Paris.

Chapter 25

Paris, April 27, 1780

Dear Nina,

I am taking the liberty of writing to Maria Theresia with you as my go-between. I am counting on your generosity and goodwill to read this letter to her.

I have let many months go by with no news because I did not know whether Maria Theresia wanted any. More-over, I did not wish to come forward while in a state of utter despondency.

After I left Vienna, I spent a long time in Switzerland. I have been living in Paris for a year, and after a difficult beginning, I am pleased to announce that the Parisians have welcomed me with open arms and have embraced my cure with great enthusiasm.

The Faculty in Vienna having warned my French colleagues of the so-called "trickery" of my method, I did not initially find here the support of doctors and scientists. Very fortunately, Doctor Charles Deslon, who tends to the Count d'Artois, brother of Louis XVI, has given me a helping hand. Failing to win the support of the Académie de Médecine of which he is a member, his friends at the Court have made a name for me and my success has been remarkable. I have been able to turn the Hôtel Bouillon on Rue Montmartre into a hospital.

Parisians are less conservative than the Viennese. They are interested in philosophy and the occult sciences. They are superstitious and fond of novelties. They are also superficial, attracted by all that glitters, provokes, and disturbs. I was thus forced to add a hefty dose of theater to my treatments and turn the magnetic cure into something more stagey. I have created a luxurious setting that corresponds not to my tastes but to those of my rich, blasé clientele, whom I am obliged to surprise and dazzle in order to make them believe in what I do. You know, dear Nina, how a patient's belief can aid in the cure. I have to nourish their desire to believe.

You saw the simplicity with which I treated our patient.
Allow me to describe the room in which I now practice. Heavy
curtains create a crepuscular half-light that is reflected in
many mirrors. Tapestries mute the sounds from outside. In the
center of the room, like a throne, is a vat, much larger than
the one you knew. An assistant demands absolute silence,
then orders the circle of patients to touch fingers. From the
distance they hear a soothing harpsichord. They become
magnetically charged without realizing it, but the intensity
of the decorum and the mystique of the atmosphere plunge
them into a state of extreme receptiveness. After an hour they
are ready to be cured. They wish to be cured. It is at this point
that I appear dressed in a full-length tunic with a steel rod in
my hand. I go from one patient to another, listening to them
describe their ills. I apply my magnetic powers to the part of
their bodies responsible for their suffering. Little by little come
the sighs and convulsions, sobbing and moaning—and in a
fit, each person rids himself of his ill and is cured.

Alas, success has its disadvantages. Mine is that I have
become too popular. My fame is harmful to my reputation.
The patients who are cured are so enthusiastic that skeptics
make fun of them, and thus of me. In Paris, magnetism is
now called "mesmerism," but the word is uttered with as
much irony as respect. For some I am a saint, a genius. For
others, I am a charlatan who takes advantage of the so-called
sick, who supposedly can snap out of their hysteria whenever

they feel like it. Some people, for example, make fun of the relaxation rooms where the men and women—mostly women—lie down after the convulsions have weakened them, and where I prefer to keep an eye on them for a few more hours. They jeer at what they think happens between me and these prostrate women. Offensive songs can be heard in the city that speak of the "mesmeromania" that has taken hold of Parisian lady folk. How can you fight against the perversities of fame? Without it, no one is interested in your work. With it, they tend to forget that your work, in fact, works. It is a vicious circle that I am powerless to stop.

I learned from my friend Moʒart that he wrote a concerto for Maria Theresia and that she is herself composing. It seems that her playing is better than ever. How has she readapted to her previous state? Is she getting treatment or has she voluntarily given up on seeing, as Moʒart seems to have suggested? When I heard this, I thought that it attested to the incredible willpower Maria Theresia has always shown.

I would like to think that her stay at Landstrasse remains for her a positive experience and that she remembers me with fond emotion, neither with bitterness nor regret.

She holds a special place in my heart.

I hope this letter finds you in good health.

Dear Nina, you have all my affection.

Franʒ Anton Mesmer

Chapter 26

Vienna, January 15, 1783

Dear Doctor Mesmer,

I was very moved by the trust your letter showed me and I thank you. I waited for a moment's quiet to read it to Maria Theresia, but she was so nervous upon learning that you had written to her that she forbade me from doing so. Many months passed until she asked me what you had to say, one evening last year.

While I was reading your letter to her, she was looking away with her hands at her eyes, so I couldn't read anything on her face. But once I finished, I saw that she was crying in silence. Tears were streaming down her face. She said nothing and asked me to write to you "when the time was right." She then locked herself in her room and I didn't see her until the next morning.

Today I decided to write to you on my own initiative, and I am sorry if you thought this letter would contain a message from Maria Theresia. In fact, she no longer wants to keep in touch with you. Several times I suggested that I answer you, but she'd put her hands to her ears the second I'd say your name and shout, "For me, he is dead!" then stop talking to me for the rest of the day. I am sorry, but I think she is determined to erase from memory this chapter in her existence.

Our life here has changed a great deal. First, we live alone in a house in the same neighborhood as Monsieur and Madame von Paradis, although they are not allowed to come visit their daughter unannounced. She has a cordial relationship with them, but something has definitively changed since their violent irruption at your home. The memory of that will never be wiped away.

Since she is blind again—which, you are right, was a voluntary decision—her life can be summed up in two words: music and piano, one being inseparable from the other. The house is awash in music and musicians. Those with whom she works, those who come to visit, those whom she teaches. It seems unbelievable, but she loves to teach beginners to play. She lays out pieces of cardboard, each of which represents a note, and with these meager tools she works miracles. She has also begun singing and composing again. Concertos, sonatas, and even an opera. Indeed, Herr Mozart did write a concerto for her, the K 456. She plays it with heartbreaking sensitivity.

She has changed considerably since her stay at your home. She is blind again, but how can I explain it? She is not like before. The innocence and candor that made her gentle and frail have now disappeared. She is extremely intense and focused, and at the same time she has a peaceful glow about her. I think she is doing exactly what she wants to be doing. She works at her music tirelessly and can pride herself on knowing by heart, without the slightest hesitation, about sixty concertos as well as a vast repertory of other pieces. All in all, more than one hundred and fifty works. She has found in this ascetic life—she repeats over and over that music is her only religion—a balance that surprises everyone she meets.

When I ask her whether she is happy with her life, she always says: "Nina, I have two pillars in my life: music and you. I know that neither of you will betray me, and this is all I need to be happy."

I pray to the heavens that this is true, that she is not just telling it to me to reassure me.

I have taken it on myself to write to you and I beg you, Herr Mesmer, not to betray me, for I am doing so only to protect her. If she learned of this letter, she might misunderstand my intentions; I would never be able to bear her distrust. This is only to show you how much I trust you.

I wanted you to hear it from me and not from others: Mademoiselle has decided to go on tour. Of course, I will be accompanying her. We are going to Bohemia, Germany, Switzerland, and then France, where we should arrive by the end of March 1784. I do not know where we will be staying, nor do I know whether you will still be in France by then, but I felt in all honesty that I had to tell you.

For weeks I have been debating the permissibility of what I am undertaking by writing you, but I ended up deciding that I owed you this show of respect.

I must ask you not to mention these projects to anyone. Organizing Maria Theresia's concert tour has been a long and complicated process, and anything can happen. If it is not a success, if she is bedridden or tired (her health is still fragile and she sometimes suffers attacks of anxiety that can paralyze her for days on end), the tour may be postponed or even cancelled.

Forgive me for having taken up so much of your time and in such a muddled fashion.

With all my respects and loyalty,

Nina

Chapter 27

IN APRIL 1784, MARIA THERESIA GAVE FOUR CONCERTS IN Paris.

The critics went into raptures over "her brilliant style," "the extreme intelligence of her playing," "her rapid and assured execution," "the lightness of her touch."

Crowds poured in to see the woman they called "the blind virtuoso." Out of pity as much as true love of music, they filled the concert halls to hear her.

On Good Friday, April 16, 1784, Maria Theresia von Paradis was the star of the Spiritual Concert, in which Mozart had triumphed six years earlier.

The concert took place before an exceptional audience of influential members of the Court and the crème de la crème of French society.

A description of this evening appears among the notes of her chambermaid, which were found in Vienna and entrusted to the music school that bears Mademoiselle Paradis's name. In these notes Nina recorded what Maria Theresia would confide to her in the dressing room after each concert.

This is what she wrote on April 16, 1784:

> *I insisted on wearing a pale pink dress because it is thanks to Marie-Antoinette's support that I was so warmly received in Paris and pink is her favorite color. I had decided to play for her. As is always the case, I dedicate each concert to someone who affects me. It can be a stranger, someone who coughs in the theater, a scent from backstage, a kind person, or a not-so-kind one, that I met the night before . . . This time it was for the Queen and I was overwhelmed, as if I'd set the bar impossibly high.*
>
> *It was an evening devoted to Mozart, and it is always a pleasure for me to play his work.*
>
> *I was led to the piano, I sat down, I felt the lights dim, and I started to play.*
>
> *I was in the middle of the fourth and last piece. Suddenly I felt a draft on my back. A wave of warmth rippled through my shoulder and down my spine. It got warmer and warmer.*

I was submerged in the heat, and for a few seconds I played better than I ever had in my whole life, with an ardor and an agility that I will never again attain.

Just before the last movement, the heat became unbearable, scalding. My temples were throbbing, my eyes twitching, and my fingers got stiff. I could no longer control them. For the first and only time in my career, I was forced to interrupt a concert.

He was in the audience.

I had felt him approach. No one had noticed him, but as soon as I stopped playing, they did. Just then, the silence in the concert hall changed. It became oppressive, unhealthy. I could feel the busybodies starting to keep score, to take bets: What would happen? Would he come up to me? Would I faint? Would we both cry?

I was thinking only of his nearness. After all these years I caught the scent of his musk and my body began to tremble. At that point, aloud, but no one could have heard me because no sound left my mouth, I said, "Good evening, Doctor Mesmer," and I started to play again.

I was able to finish the sonata, but I did not do the encore with which I usually close each concert. When I stood up for the applause, I felt him walking away. He was taking with him the memory of a love. Of an illusion.

Chapter 28

FRANZ ANTON MESMER NEVER RECEIVED RECOGNITION from France for his discovery of animal magnetism. In 1784, at the request of Louis XVI, a commission led by Benjamin Franklin was established to study the phenomenon. It concluded that because magnetism could not be observed directly, its existence could not be proved. Mesmer was officially declared an impostor.

He left France in 1785 and returned to his place of birth near Lake Constance. He died of a heart attack on March 5, 1815.

Maria Theresia gave concerts across Europe and met with enormous success in both Paris and London.

In 1785, she returned to Vienna, where she devoted herself mostly to composing. She wrote five operas, six concertos, twelve sonatas, plus cantatas and chamber music.

In 1800, she began teaching. She created a music school for girls in Vienna in 1808.

It is there that she died on February 1, 1824, in her sleep.